Behind the Door II: Revelation Revealed

Honney Lavern Barner

Contact Dr. Honney Lavern Barner

Email - behindthedoor2018@gmail.com

Facebook Page - Behind the Door: The Secrets to the Beginning

Behind the Door II: Revelation Revealed (Release - May 2019)

Behind the Door III: Revelation Unleashed (Release – April 2020)

RCS Publishing

rcspublishingandmedia@gmail.com

This story was written to all the leaders who serve in our government:

To the President of the United States – You are the President for ALL Americans.

To the Congress – never sacrifice integrity to win.

To the Senate – serve with, integrity, dignity and respect for the rule of law.

To the Supreme Court – God empowered you to make the law – Do it fairly.

To the State level leadership – serve your communities with honesty, compassion, and respect for the needs of those who put you in office.

To the Armed Forces – Thank you for your Service.

And to all those who have influence on society and profit from our democracy:

To the Movie Industry – you can destroy the hearts and minds of God's people – just because you can do it doesn't mean you should.

To the Music Industry – words are powerful – be careful about what you say.

To the Business Industry – never put profits before integrity, honesty, and fairness.

To the Financial Industry – when enough is enough – don't allow power and greed to win.

To the Professional Sports Industry – you do influence our children – honor that.

To the Career Professionals – You will be accountable for your service – serve well.

Dedication

The Behind the Door Trilogy is dedicated to:

Jesus Christ, My Lord and Savior.

LTC (retired) Franchestee J. Barner, my beloved wife and best friend and inspiration to write this trilogy.

2nd LT Haven L. Barner, my awesome son, graduate of United States Military Academy, West Point, NY.

Gabriella M. Barner, my talented superstar daughter, freshman at Mountain View High School, VA.

Thanks to all the women that prayed and poured into my life and made me the man I am today: My one of a kind mother Alice M. Barner, grandmother Emma Everette, my aunts Chris White & Shirley Christian, and my super-fantastic mother-in-laws Maria Ruth McNair, and Rachel McCleese.

And to "You" the Reader...

Thank you!

Acknowledgements

I acknowledge God, and He is God all by Himself; He is the Creator to the world; He is the Alpha and Omega; He is the first and the last; He is the beginning and the end; He is the God of Gods, Lord of Lords, King of Kings; He is the God of Abraham, Isaac, and Jacob; He is the God of Israel; He is the Great "I AM".

I acknowledge Jesus Christ as my Lord and my Savior.

I acknowledge the Holy Spirit as my Guide and my Comforter.

I acknowledge RCS publishing for their amazing talent, commitment to perfection, dedication unlike anything I have ever experienced, and the steady inspiration and motivation to see and understand my vision for this novel.

I acknowledge all the readers of Behind the Door I – The Secrets to the Beginning. Thanks for making my very first novel an Amazon Best Seller, Most Gifted, and #1 Released. Let's do it again with Behind the Door II – Revelation Unleashed.

I acknowledge all the venues, businesses, churches, universities and homes that invited me to come share my story and hosting book signings.

I acknowledge all the guests on my weekly Podcast "Dr. Honney Lavern Barner, Hour of Power." Thanks for sharing your heart, faith, and beliefs about "What if there is No God and What if there is a God? A very special thanks to my international guest from Portugal, France, Germany, England, Iceland, and the island of Lajes.

It was an amazing experience for my family and me to travel to these wonderful countries and meet the amazing people who also shared their faith and beliefs about the Most High God.

Prologue

Gazing down from the 10th floor he could see the crowd expand, seemingly multiplying from hundreds of people to thousands right before his eyes. The people were holding signs and singing hymns that suddenly warmed him from the inside. They sang songs that he recalled from his youth choir days at, Living Waters Baptist Church.

A lonely tear traveled down his cheek.

Those were the greatest times of his life. Thoughts of his father began to crowd his mind as he suddenly felt the floor drop beneath him.

He was falling...

Darkness surrounded him as he felt his body sinking.

"Help!" he screamed as he tumbled down an endless hole pleading for someone to rescue him, but to no avail. His words seemed to be muffled by the sound of collapsing dirt and debris.

He outstretched his arms to try and slow his fall, but only managed to cover himself with dirt in the process.

He closed his eyes and prayed for protection.

Clawing at the red clay that surrounded the walls of the pit, he tried to see if there was a way out. His hands dug deep into the earth, he could feel the dirt beneath his fingernails, clogging his nails, making his hands feel heavier somehow.

Hot tears flowed down his cheeks as he considered his own demise. He was going to die here and no one would even know. Images of his daughters, his wife and his mother's face crowded his mind. He couldn't leave them alone like this. His mother wouldn't survive having to bury her own son. He felt horrible, how could this be happening?

"Someone help me" he continued to scream although he knew that no one would hear him.

He was in the middle of nowhere at a precarious time of the night. The silence of the starry skied night reminded him that he was alone.

No one was around, he was helpless and he knew it.

He tried to position his body to prevent the inevitable gravitational pull to the ground, but none came. He continued to fall in the void, feeling his body give way as he screamed for help.

A blinding light pierced through the darkness, illuminating the ground below and quickening his heart rate. The bright light reflected and bounced off of something that caught his eye. Intrigued he reached out and touched the brightly decorated door gasping in awe. He couldn't believe it, he found a door.

Rubbing his hands over the door he could feel the impressions of carved symbols, fascinated by what he saw before him he stood and tried to feel for the doorknob. As soon as his hand touched the door he was struck with a stream of hallucinations.

Images flashed before him as his awareness began to intensify. People were openly and carelessly committing crimes. Sin was rampant. He watched as crowds of people torched famed churches and mosques. He sighed with deep pain as he watched the world burn. Jonathan watched a crowd of torch wielding, hate mongers chanting, "White Power". He witnessed the crowd beat and pummel everyone within their reach who didn't look like them.

Tears streamed down his cheeks as he watched children wandering helplessly, searching for direction or an authority figure, but there were none. Men held other men in their arms, seductively embracing wearing looks of longing and passion.

That's when his father's face appeared. A curly mop of blonde hair, bright blue eyes dancing around happily and a warm smile spread broadly across his face, just as Jonathan remembered. His father's face eased his mind, giving Jonathan a glimmer of hope.

"You must warn them," he said reaching out to him.

"Dad!" Jonathan cried as he reached for his father in vain. Brad Flannigan reached out towards his son and mouthed, "You must warn them…," he repeated in a much softer voice as his image began to dissipate.

Jonathan could feel the tears streaming down his cheeks as he cried for his father.

"Dad!" Jonathan screamed, hoping to hear his father's voice again. He knew that it was all a dream but it didn't matter. Seeing his father again was worth more than gold to him. He knew that it was something that wouldn't happen.

Jonathan was a senior in high school when his father met his untimely death in a car accident on an excavation mission abroad. He thought about his father daily. His father was such a strong influence on him that although he was no longer physically there Jonathan used most of his wisdom and guidance from his formative years to lead him.

It had been nearly two decades since Jonathan's father spoke to him. He missed hearing his voice. He craved his father's touch. Jonathan continued to call his father's name but he knew that Brad was long gone and Jonathan was alone again.

He suddenly felt a hand on his shoulder, shaking him from his nightmare. "Jonathan, are you alright?" his wife asked with concern in her eyes. Fighting back tears, he shook his head in confusion.

Jonathan was far from okay, he was terrified.

Psalm 91:2

"I will say of the Lord, He is my refuge and my fortress: my God; In him will I trust."

Chapter 1

Angela smiled as the rays of sunshine beamed through the kitchen window warming the side of her face. She slowly sipped Chamomile tea from her favorite mug, marked "Nana". She stared blankly at the newspaper article as her mind drifted to a place where it often visited, a place she'd come to recognize as panic-inducing.

Taking a deep breath, she closed her eyes and whispered her favorite verse to settle her thoughts. Psalm 91 – *"Whoever dwells in the shelter of the Most High will rest in the shadow of the Almighty. I will say of the Lord, "He is my refuge and my fortress, my God, in him will I trust."*

"I trust you, Lord," she said as she completed the entire verse from memorization. After the death of her husband, Angela learned to lean on the word of God like never before.

Tall, slim with shoulder length gray hair, Angela Flannigan was a beautiful woman who had experienced her fair share of heart wrenching moments that forced her to her knees in prayer. She had also seen joy and felt love so deep that she not only survived her life's traumas, she thrived in spite of them.

After dedicating nearly forty years to the Children's Ministry at The Living Waters Baptist Church she finally retired leaving her schedule open for fun and excitement, so she thought.

Angela was growing increasingly stir crazy and found herself searching for something to place her attention. Lately, she found herself reviewing all of the information associated with Jonathan's adventure in Jerusalem. Although the entire experience made her nervous, once he came home he was so excited about his journey that Angela couldn't help but become equally enthralled with everything.

Watching his blue eyes bounce around as he described his time exploring the last place that his father walked. Angela didn't understand, initially, in fact she was angry with her son for deciding on a whim to pack up and leave his family for such a dangerous journey. She didn't tell Jonathan, but she was upset that he would decide to go back to the place that she tried her hardest to forget.

It wasn't that she didn't want him to see Ashkelon, Jerusalem she just wanted to be made aware of it. A mother never stopped being a mother, even when her son was well into his 30s. She prayed for Jonathan and his family daily, sometimes more than once a day because he needed the added protection. She just wished that he kept her in the loop.

Only a few months had passed since her son flew into town with a solid story and his bright smile. She and Kelly questioned him nonstop, but he said nothing beyond the fact that he had to gain closure. She couldn't believe that he went that far for closure but Angela couldn't blame her son.

After suffering the loss of her husband so long ago she still felt the grief and sadness as raw as the day she found out that he wouldn't be returning from Ashkelon. The fact that her son went to the same place without her knowledge unsettled her.

In fact, the whole situation did. It bothered her to no end, but her son was a grown man and he had already made his decision.

He told her that he went on a journey to find himself; he wanted to be a better man for his family; for Angela. She tried to tell Jonathan that he already made her extremely proud.

He was a self-sufficient man with a loving family that was all Angela could ask for. She let it go, but there was something in Luke's eyes that said there was more to the story than she was being told. Angela assured herself that she would find out what really happened to her son so she could better support him. She was an analytical thinker, someone who endeavored to get to the bottom of things.

Angela enjoyed solving puzzles and something told her that Jonathan's situation was equally as puzzling as the game she glanced at on the table in front of her.

After preparing every meal she could think of and spoiling him as much as she could, she kissed her son and his family, "good-bye" wiped away lonely tears and watched them board the Amtrak train.

She missed her son and wanted to hop in the car and visit him, but she had to remind herself that Jonathan and his family was hundreds of miles away in New York City. He promised her that he would return home for Christmas vacation, but the summer heat outside of Angela's window reminded her that her son's visit would be months away.

Taking a deep breath, she made a decision. "I am going to New York," she declared placing the mug of tea on the table next to the article with her handsome son's smile on the page.

Psalm 91:5

"Thou shalt not be afraid for the terror by night; [nor] for the arrow [that] flieth by day."

Chapter 2

Sitting up in the bed, sweating profusely Jonathan tried to calm his pounding heart. He quickly glanced at his wife to be sure that his nightmare didn't wake her. Kelly's long blonde hair hung around her shoulders as she slept peacefully. He was grateful that he didn't wake her. She seemed to sleep through anything lately. Sleep was the one thing that eluded him, however.

His nightmares were increasing in frequency.

Nearly a year had passed since his trip to Jerusalem. Jonathan was still haunted by reoccurring nightmares. He would've written the nightmares off as PTSD suffered from his experience in Ashkelon, but there was one big issue.

The nightmares weren't centered on his fall in Jerusalem.

They involved his father. His father had been deceased for decades and it unnerved Jonathan that he was making reappearance in his dreams.

The last time his father visited his dreams he had a plan for Jonathan. He wondered what his father's visit meant this time. It saddened him that he couldn't talk to his father any longer or hear his voice. The hardest part of his nightmares was the fact that he couldn't share them with anyone.

The last thing he wanted to do was bother his wife or his mother about his nightmares. He thought about his grandfather. He would help Jonathan find a scripture to interpret his dream, but Jonathan cringed at the thought of contacting him.

It wasn't that he didn't trust his grandfather. He loved and valued his grandfather, but he didn't want to stress his grandfather unnecessarily. The situation in Jerusalem was far more than he wanted to put on the older man.

When he was in Jerusalem, Robert told him that he contacted his grandfather and was preparing to send him home comfortably, Jonathan smiled. He knew that his grandfather wanted to fly there to be sure that he was alright. Instead, his grandfather made sure that he returned home safely with only a few healing scratches and bruises.

His grandfather told Kelly and Angela just enough to keep them informed, but they didn't know the complexities of Jonathan's situation in Jerusalem. He could imagine his mother never allowing him to leave Minnesota if she knew how grave his situation was in Jerusalem.

The matriarch of the Flannigan family was as much strong and determined as she was beautiful and delicate. Angela was not one to underestimate. Brad used to warn about his wife being a "quiet storm". Brad was the only person who could get away with teasing Angela and making her giggle with amusement.

He longed for those days again. Now his father visited him only in his dreams.

Brad Flannigan was a mere apparition an image that both relieved and disturbed Jonathan. As a child, he adored his father. A world-renowned archeologist and not to mention one of the most caring people Jonathan had ever met, his father was his everything. He taught Jonathan how to be a man.

Jonathan's entire life changed the day his father died. He started on a path that was checkered with drug abuse, alcohol binging and rebellious behavior and denying his faith. It took the tough love from his grandfather, Pastor Luke Flannigan to pull him out of the depths of despair.

Jonathan was forever grateful to his grandfather for not giving up on him. He bailed him out of situations that Jonathan tried hard to forget about. His grandfather never judged him or condemned his coming of age antics. He simply loved him. That was all Jonathan needed in his life, to be assured that he was loved in spite of his mistakes.

Both his mother and his grandfather did just that.

It was Luke's dedication to Jonathan's future that ultimately set his life on a new course. He owed his grandfather a great deal of gratitude, but he didn't want to bring this concern to his grandfather. For once he would handle things on his own without involving his grandfather.

Jonathan made up his mind about his next steps before the sun rose the next morning. He would just have to plan everything out properly in order to execute without a hitch. He couldn't afford to have any snafus this time and he definitely couldn't afford to be placed in a life challenging situation.

John 14:1

"Let not your hearts be troubled. Believe in God; believe also in me."

Chapter 3

"Please stow away your carry-on items and place your seats in the upright positions as we prepare for landing," the flight attendant requested as Dr. Wellington folded the Science Daily magazine and slid it inside his brown leather carryon bag. He peeked through the open shade and smiled at the city below. "Different city, different experiences," he said to himself as he imagined what would await him in Guatemala.

He was on a mission to locate ancient artifacts inside the ancient metropolis of Kaminaljuyú. Excavated in the late 1930s, the place was filled with artifacts that held nearly 1,500 years worth of history. He was excited to begin this new excavation, but he couldn't keep his mind off that fateful day.

Images of his friend and confidant, Brad Flannigan flashed before his eyes. He missed his dear friend. Robert Wellington was struggling with a guilt buried so deep within his heart he feared he'd never overcome the feeling. It had been so long since he had a restful sleep, enjoyed a great meal, and even longer since he had a decent date.

Robert Wellington was a shell of a man.

Seeing Brad's son was surreal for Robert. The young man reminded Robert of his father when they first began working for the University of Minnesota.

As hard as he tried he couldn't get the image of the red car careening towards them that night. He couldn't get the sound of tires screaming as the collision shattered not only his life but also so many others whom Brad touched.

Brad saved his life!

His best friend died saving his life. Robert would never be the same. It bothered him to no end that he nearly caused the demise of Brad's only son in the same place nearly two decades later. It broke his heart to make the phone call to Luke Flannigan's home.

It was the worst type of déjà vu, he felt horrible.

To his dismay, Luke found himself consoling Robert after his best friend's death. Robert didn't tell anyone but Brad's death was a defining moment in his life. He found himself at a crossroads. After decades of establishing his career and professional standing in the world of archeology he was prepared to walk away from it all.

Everything he did reminded him of Brad. Every time he conducted the radiocarbon dating process for an artifact he remembered conversations that he had with Brad about simplifying the process. He was still doing it his way. He chuckled to himself thinking about the look Brad had on his face as he watched his friend go through the process, taking the extra steps that he somehow managed to avoid.

Brad's death shook Robert to his core. Robert knew that losing Brad had a devastating affect on his family, as well. Family was Brad's top priority. Brad was always there for Robert, even when he felt discouraged. Brad was there replaying a recorded sermon delivered by his father, Luke. Luke's calm and striking voice had a way of soothing and encouraging Robert to continue on. Brad remarked about his son, Jonathan's enthusiasm towards archeology. Robert smiled to himself as he recalled Brad's eagerness to bring his son, Jonathan along on an expedition. It was all he talked about. They were both looking forward to an archeological dig with Pastor Flannigan in tow.

Robert shook his head ferociously as the image of Luke's grief stricken face haunted his thoughts.

After he assisted Luke with returning Brad's remains home, he decided to take a break altogether. His colleagues understood. The site actually shut down for several days after Brad's death. Robert left town for nearly a week before returning to complete his obligations.

He busied himself with cataloging the items that were located in the dig, but he knew deep down that things would never be the same on the sites that he worked. Brad's footprint was on everything. From the sifting trays that bore his name to his lucky pickax that Robert lovingly handed over to his son Jonathan.

The excavation assignment concluded several months later and Robert skipped town as soon as he could. He found himself on an island in the Caribbean relaxing at a hotel overlooking the sea. The bright sky and blue water were in strong contrast to his melancholy mood, but he was determined to heal from the events surrounding Brad's tragic death.

His friend couldn't die in vain!

He never told anyone, but he received a letter the day that Brad arrived in Ashkelon. Engulfed in the excitement and splendor of the moment he didn't think anything of the letter warning him to cancel the excavation and leave the holy land at once.

Robert brushed the letter off as mere intimidation tactics that came along with the job. Every archeologist had experienced it. They talked about it constantly in both academia and in personal gatherings. Some citizens didn't want archeological excavations on their land. They felt that the digs were dishonoring their ancient history and destroying the land that their ancestors dwelled on for centuries.

Robert understood their plight, but he also knew that there was no better way to piece together the ancient history of past civilizations than by excavating. Persuading someone to look on the other side of something that they felt passionate about was rarely an easy task.

No one wanted to hear his explanations. They just wanted them off their land. Robert regretted not saying anything. He wondered if his friend would have been alive if he would have simply heeded the warnings that he received. He mulled over the decision to involve Brad in the Ashkelon excavation for weeks.

It was Dr. Fry who ultimately convinced him to toss aside his fears concerning the dig and invite Brad along. He knew that Lawrence Fry was determined to find something substantial in the Jerusalem dig. Not only did he help fund the dig he also included a substantial bonus for Robert with only one stipulation, he must bring Brad Flannigan along.

It didn't seem like such an odd request to Robert at first. Brad was one of the best in the field. His name graced many magazine covers and he taught Archeology at the University of Minnesota. It wasn't until protestors flooded their dig site that first night that Robert began to question the motives of Dr. Fry.

When Robert voiced his concerns over safety issues in the city he brushed them aside with an inconsequential wave. He smiled at Robert and gave him a pat on the back, "everything will be fine," he assured.

Everything was far from fine, however. Losing Brad was devastating. It was in the warm salty waters of Lindquist Beach that Robert was able to restore himself. Robert dove in the water daily and floated along with the current as it drifted out to the rock wall barriers leading to the ocean.

It wasn't until he saw Jonathan resting in the hospital bed in Ashkelon that he realized how dangerous his decision to bring him back to the excavation site was. When he was initially approached by Dr. Fry about revisiting the site, he declined the offer.

Money, however was a great encourager and Dr. Fry spared no expense in his effort to win Dr. Wellington over. Robert Wellington took the money graciously, and packed his belongings as he set out on a trip of a lifetime. He was determined to get Jonathan out to Jerusalem. He brought his friend's only son out to Jerusalem and they almost lost him.

He couldn't believe the shock in Luke Flannigan's voice when he told him that Jonathan was a bit battered and bruised but he was resting comfortably. Luke didn't know that his grandson was halfway across the globe on an excavation trip, but he didn't miss a beat.

Robert felt the fear in Luke's voice as he told him that they pulled his grandson out of a hole after 24 hours. He sobbed with gratitude and joy when he told him that Jonathan was doing well. He asked that Robert keep him posted on his well being. He also requested one thing of Robert Wellington, that he not contact anyone else with Jonathan's whereabouts or condition.

Robert couldn't forgive himself for putting Jonathan in danger, so although the request sounded strange, he honored it.

Daniel 2:28

"But there is a God in heaven that revealeth secrets, and maketh known to the king Nebuchadnezzar what shall be in the latter days. Thy dream, and the visions of thy head upon thy bed, are these."

Chapter 4

Jonathan groaned as he tried to clear his mind of the horrible visions. Every night his sleep was interrupted by nightmares. His dreams were growing more and more vivid. Jonathan felt like he was committing a sin every moment that he wasn't doing what God called him to do.

The reporters were going wild. An earthquake occurred in Western Maryland. There hadn't been an earthquake in that region in decades. At the same time reports were coming in from India about a devastating tsunami.

The book of Revelations was playing out in Jonathan's dream, once again. Death, disease and famine were all around him. California was experiencing the worst drought in history, due to wildfires, while the southern area of the United States were hit with floods.

Jonathan let out a loud sigh and sat up in the bed.

When he finally opened his eyes, Jonathan checked online to see if the things he envisioned in his dreams were real. He breathed a sigh of relief when he located the national news website and didn't find anything about earthquakes or tsunamis.

Jonathan closed his eyes in a feigned attempt to ignore the madness occurring directly in front of him. New York City had no shortage of strange happenings, but everything seemed to be falling apart at the seams. He was still reeling from the latest news story about the plight to legalize gay marriage.

The discussion on the television had captured so much of his attention, he was now late for his first appointment. As he hurried down the sidewalk, he suddenly came to a stop. A happy couple were engaged in a heated, passionate kiss in the middle of the sidewalk. He cleared his throat trying to get their attention. He just needed them to step aside so he could get by. When they turned to face him, he gasped.

Disappointed in the scene before him, Jonathan shook his head sadly at the two men. He couldn't judge the individuals but the gay marriage topic weighed extra heavy on his mind after he witnessed the scene. Two of his coworkers had emerged from the "closet" about their sexual preferences in the law firm.

It didn't bother Jonathan that their preferences were different than his own. He was more annoyed that the world had become a place where individuals felt emboldened to share their sexual conquests with anyone and everyone.

He thought about the world that his daughters were forced to grow up in and it made him feel sad. It unnerved Jonathan that he couldn't turn on the television or leave his home without being reminded that the world was growing consumed with their own sins.

Jonathan passed by several people on the street who were passed out. Judging by their un-kept appearance and the way everyone stepped over them, Jonathan was sure that they were struggling with either addiction or mental issues. He had seen his fair share of drug addicted individuals in the Big Apple.

Mental illness was looked at even worse than drug abuse. Since many institutions and mental hospitals were closed, scores of the mentally ill were left to manage their symptoms on their own. Jonathan passed the homeless people on the street and felt horrible for them. While there were intervention programs in the City many of the direct public were oblivious to the misery surrounding them.

Addiction was such a sad sight. It is a disease that does not pick and choose who it affects. Addiction stole mothers, fathers and grandparents from families; leaving them to the streets. It grieved Jonathan that those walking on the street ignored the addicted and the hungry as they hurried to their high paying jobs.

He dropped a five dollar bill in the hand of a mother holding a crying infant, begging for money. Jonathan watched as the people behind him walked past the woman, ignoring her pain.

Did anyone care?

"God, something needs to be done," he cried out as he walked to his job. "Please, God. Your people are suffering," he said as visions of the hungry and depressed flooded his mind. Jonathan held out his hand and steadied himself on the bench nearby. He took in deep breaths, trying his best to regain his composure.

Everything around him seemed to overwhelm him. He sat down on the bench and closed his eyes for a brief minute. The moment his eyes closed he saw visions of world burning. He saw children crying begging for help as their parents shot drugs in their arms, right in front of them. Jonathan groaned as visions of people storming and burning churches, synagogues and religious buildings.

The visions came rapidly as Jonathan grew nauseous from the thought of it all. The world was on a rapid downward spiral and he had to find a way to stop it all. Jonathan opened his eyes and let out a breath. He had to warn them all, if he didn't the world would be destroyed just like Sodom and Gomorrah. The ancient city of the New Testament that was so consumed by sin, God showed his wrath and rained down destruction.

Jonathan wondered how he could stop it. He could not believe how the food industry was using so many pesticides and chemicals on our food which was causing the largest outbreak of cancer, diabetics, high blood pressures and more. It appeared to him that the medical community and the food industry were working in concert with each other. The medical community was acting like " legal drug dealers" getting people hooked on drugs. The opioid crisis was exploding throughout the United States. The young and old were becoming addicted to this legal drug.

He had to convince everyone to repent of their sins so that they could be forgiven and saved. If not they would face the same destruction that those of Sodom and Gomorrah faced.

Could America be next?

The book of Revelations was unfolding in front of him. Jonathan tried to ignore everything that was happening around him, but he knew that it was impossible. He had to warn the world of their impending danger. Their only solution was to repent of their sins and ask for forgiveness. He would tell the world and try to save as many as he possibly could.

Luke 12:15

"And he said unto them, Take heed, and beware of covetousness: for a man's life consisteth not in the abundance of the things which he possesseth."

Chapter 5

The sun blazed overhead conveying the illusion of waves dancing before his eyes. Shielding his eyes from the blinding sun, he let out a loud sigh. Five months in the desert searching for an ancient burial ground and he was exhausted. He couldn't stop, though. He would never stop. Staring out into the vast sea of scorching sand he nodded in affirmation.

There was something out there and he was determined to find it.

Holding the notebook in his sweaty hands he stared at the hand drawn, worn map, squinting at the writing. Yellowed and weathered by years of manipulation the map was barely legible, but he memorized everything. Years of obsessing over the buried treasure seared the map in his memory.

Dr. Lawrence Fry was on a mission and nothing would stop him this time.

The coordinates on his GPS tracker began to spell out the exact location of his treasure. After years of searching and committing acts that he never thought he would do, he was finally in possession of the map.

He secretly hoped that his reliance on Brad's expertise wasn't a mistake. Lawrence hoped that Brad wrote the coordinates down properly, but he knew that Brad Flannigan was a stringent, calculated man when it came to research. He had more than enough faith in Brad's work, ample faith to pack up his belongings and trek back out to Ashkelon to search for it.

Reading Brad's handwriting, Lawrence tried to shake his last memory of his old colleague before he died. His last remembrance of Brad wasn't a good one. Brad's usual gentle, calm demeanor was replaced with a concerned scowl as he explained to Lawrence that he would not pursue the treasure hunt with him. He called it a "mercenary mission," which infuriated Lawrence.

Brad glared at Lawrence with confusion in his eyes. "This is the type of thing that my father and I fight against. So, we're resorting to flat out robbery, Lawrence? This is not what you brought me out here for," he questioned with an angry whisper. His behavior was a stark contrast to the *Brad Flannigan* that everyone knew and loved.

How dare Brad lecture him on morality?

True, the great theologian Luke Flannigan was every bit of the encourager and motivator that everyone claimed him to be, but he wasn't God. Lawrence made sure he reminded Brad of that fact during their heated conversation that fateful evening, twenty years ago.

The memory was decades old, but remained fresh in his mind. Lawrence recalled the way his blood boiled as Brad accused him of grave robbing. He wanted to punch the smug young man, but instead, he devised a different plan.

A plan that haunted him every night.

Lawrence was preoccupied by the images of Brad being thrown to the ground by the impact of his red car. No one would ever know that he was driving the red car that careened into both Brad and Robert Wellington that fateful night. They would never understand how desperate Lawrence felt when he decided to kill his colleagues. Since neither men decided to go along with his treasure hunt he knew that it would have only been a matter of time before they turned him in.

He couldn't risk it.

It didn't take him long to secure himself behind the wheel of the vehicle. The hard part was leaving the scene just as quickly as he arrived upon it. The sound of bones and carnage under his mangled car still permeated his thoughts. He watched Robert and Brad's bodies lying still and lifeless on the ground. At the moment of impact his eyes locked with Robert Wellington's.

Lawrence didn't stick around to see if both men died in the crash. He secretly hoped that they were both dead as he slid out of the car and hobbled away from the crash, disappearing from sight. He thought he got away with murder, but he realized soon after that he didn't really get away with anything. Lawrence could escape the prosecution from the accident but he knew that he couldn't escape judgment.

He was a shell of a man now, he barely ate and very rarely slept. How could he?

That night haunted his memories and Brad haunted his dreams. Decades later, he still wondered if Robert knew that it was him who tried to kill them both. Lawrence was tormented, but still determined.

At times it seemed as if Lawrence would give in to his conscious and turn himself in to the authorities. But his greed and determination to discover the find of a life time were much deeper in the darkest corner of his soul.

Hebrews 3:13

"Help each other. Speak day after day to each other while it is still today so your heart will not become hard by being fooled by sin."

Chapter 6

"Help me," he heard as he ran through the desert searching for the voice. "I'm coming," he called out as the hot sand scorched the pads of his feet causing him to grimace in pain. He didn't care about the searing sun or the heat beneath his feet he was on a mission that even pain wouldn't stop.

He ran with a purpose, feet digging into the sand; tossing the grain against his bare legs as he pushed himself. He had to reach the terrified voice that he heard in the distance.

Suddenly, the smell of salty sea air hit his nose and he stopped to decipher the smell.

"Help!" the plead continued as he wiped the sweat from his brow. "I'm coming, son" he yelled just as he reached his grandson sinking in a sea of rough waves. Astonished at the sight of the ocean in the middle of the scorching hot desert he rubbed his eyes and dove into the gurgling, violent sea.

He pumped his arms and legs with a fierceness trying his hardest to reach Jonathan as quickly as his body would allow. As he swam towards his grandson, the young boy continued to float further away from him. He tried to yell to the boy that he was coming, but he couldn't catch his breath.

The ocean began to swell and rise in front of them, moving towards them at lightening speed, threatening to engulf everything in its path. The fear in his heart didn't stop him from trying to save his grandson. He finally reached Jonathan just as the wave crest high above them and suddenly came crashing down on top of them both.

"No!" he screamed as he sat up in the middle of his bed. Looking around in astonishment he was relieved to see that the ocean waves threatening to engulf him were replaced by plush white bedding and mint green walls. He was back in his bedroom. Glancing at the clock he let out an exasperated sigh. It was only 2:00 am in the morning. He desperately needed to get some sleep.

Every night for the past several weeks he had been jolted awake by the same nightmare.

Deep down inside Luke Flannigan knew that his dreams had to mean something but he couldn't remember the dream in detail to decipher it.

That truly bothered Luke. The only thing that jumped out to him was the fact that his grandson needed him. He could feel it in his heart.

Climbing out of bed and falling to his knees he did what he had been doing for weeks, he began to pray. "Dear Lord, I come to you humbly thanking you for showing me the signs that I need to see for my family's sake. Lord, I ask that you calm my heart and my thoughts so that I may fully understand what it is that you would like me to do. Whatever you ask of me, father, I will do," he said as he continued to meditate and savor his quiet time with God.

His many years of studying the scripture taught him that God spoke to His people often; it was up to His followers to hear His voice. Pastor Luke made it a point to pause after he prayed, to allow silence so he could clearly hear God's voice.

"Whatever you need me to do, I will do," he said as he slowly climbed from his kneeling position to sit in the bed. He opened his Bible to the Old Testament and began to read Genesis 40. Although, he read the book many times before he was always intrigued by Joseph's story, especially when he had bad dreams.

Joseph was a dedicated follower of God. His gift was interpreting dreams. The gift that God blessed him with took him from prison to the king's trusted council. Joseph possessed a gift and so did Pastor Luke. He just had to be patient and wait on God to reveal his full intentions through his dreams.

Luke held on to the Bible like a lifeline. He clutched it close to his chest and closed his eyes, simply meditating on the scriptures he just read.

Flipping to the book of Hebrews he read the scripture aloud, "You must warn each other every day, while it is still "today," so that none of you will be deceived by sin and hardened against God." – Hebrews 3:13 NLT

The longer he reflected on the scripture in front of him, the more assured he grew about what he had to do.

Psalm 46:1

"God is our safe place and our strength. He is always our help when we are in trouble."

Chapter 7

Kelly Flannigan circled the room with her hands in the air, in confusion. She went into Brittany's room to retrieve something but had completely forgotten what she was searching for. Laughing to herself, she sat down on Brittany's pink daisy imprinted bed to give herself a moment to just breathe.

It seemed like she had been burning the candle at both ends lately. She was growing increasingly tired.

Brittany called out from the bottom of the stairs asking her mother if she located the ribbon for her dance competition. Smiling to herself she said aloud, "Aha" reaching in the top drawer to pull out the ribbon. She ran around so much she couldn't keep up with her own thoughts.

She had to drop her daughters off at dance rehearsal for their evening competition and then she had to run back to her office to show her clients an elegant luxury high rise apartment on the upper west side. Kelly loved her job.

After five years in Real Estate she truly found her niche. She walked away from her sales position in the corporate world to spend more time with her family. Realty was the key to her work and home life balance.

She wouldn't have it any other way.

Kelly needed to experience a different side of life. She enjoyed being a Realtor. Matching prospective owners with their dream home was truly fulfilling for her. She remembered her first sale. After the closing meeting she went in the restroom and cried like a baby. She was so overjoyed and filled with the spirit of gratitude.

She wasn't a religious person by any stretch of the imagination but she knew that her luck was finally turning up. Smiling to herself she armed the alarm in their apartment and called out to the girls, "ladies, it's time to roll," she said as the sound of four tiny feet stampeding across the hallway floor made her laugh.

Watching her girls hold hands as they headed towards the awaiting elevator she was overcome with happiness. She loved her life.

Helping the girls in the car she pulled out into traffic ready to start her day. Brianna and Brittany were singing nursery rhymes that they had remixed into their own funny versions. They were tickled laughing in the back seat as she drove to the dance school.

Once Kelly dropped the girls off at class, she headed to meet her client. Driving in Manhattan was not something that she enjoyed doing, but she had to meet her client and she was determined to get there on time. The trains were unpredictable and she enjoyed the solitude of being in her own vehicle alone.

She turned the music up and began to drive the short distance to the apartment complex. It took less than twenty minutes to reach her destination, which was quite surprising in New York traffic. She eased her Volvo 760 into the small area marked "valet" and climbed out of the car with ease.

When she reached the inside of the building she took a deep breath. It seemed to take her forever to reach the inside of the large building. Once she entered she smiled with great satisfaction. Her client would love this place. The white marble flooring and the rich mahogany wood accented with gold trimmings, this place was luxury at its finest.

She felt her phone vibrating in her pocket and glanced down at the message, "I'm here" she responded with a kissing emoji and another of a house telling Jonathan that she arrived at her first house visit. Since their schedules varied she rarely saw her husband before the late evening hours. They checked in with each other via text message throughout the day.

"Mrs. Flannigan," she heard from behind as she turned to face her client, Harold Ting. Mr. Ting was a businessman from China purchasing property for his twin daughters who would be attending NYU in the fall. He wanted them to have a comfortable place to call home when they grew tired of their dormitories.

Kelly had the pleasure of scoping out perspective apartments for her young adult clients. She was happy with this place. Breathtaking views of both Central Park and Manhattan were the reason why she decided to show the apartment to Mr. Ting.

The luxury digs would win the girls over immediately, but their bedrooms were the real winners. Oversized floor to ceiling windows, open floor plan and granite countertops made this place look like a palace.

She shook Mr. Ting's hand and escorted him to the elevator so they could check out the home on the fourth floor. Mr. Ting didn't say much during the ride up to the apartment, instead Kelly talked about the particulars concerning the home.

"You will be happy to find that this home has three bedrooms, three full baths and a full kitchen. There is access to the pool on the third floor and the fitness room on the first floor. A personal concierge is on staff to meet all of their needs. I really think your girls will love this place," she said as the elevator dinged signaling their arrival.

The sweeping views of the city were displayed at every turn through massive windows. With over 2,000 square feet of luxury this apartment was larger than Kelly and her husband's first home.

Kelly couldn't imagine living in this apartment as a recent high school graduate, especially with parents living abroad. The Ting girls were wealthy from birth. It was an interesting dynamic that intrigued Kelly.

She reached the heavy wooden door and used her key to open it. When the door opened to reveal the sheer awesomeness of the room, Mr. Ting let out a slow whistle. She smiled to herself knowing that the sale was secured.

Kelly walked inside the living room and spun around with her arms high in the air. "Please take a moment to look around and get yourself familiar with this lovely place," she said just before becoming overtaken by a coughing spell.

Kelly's coughing fit lasted so long Mr. Ting ran to the kitchen and grabbed a glass out of the cupboard to fill with water from the sink. She didn't realize what was happening until he handed her the glass. Kelly couldn't catch her breath.

After several minutes of sipping the water and slowing her breathing, she was finally able to move from the couch. She quickly apologized to her client who wouldn't hear anything of her apology. They continued to survey the luxurious fourth floor apartment. Kelly showed Mr. Ting every amenity available in the luxury home.

Proverbs 18:10

"The name of the **Lord** is a strong tower; the righteous run into it and are safe."

Chapter 8

Jonathan leaned back in his seat and stretched his arms out as he yawned. He was exhausted. The door swung open as his first client entered wearing a look of pure anguish. Jonathan knew that this case was going to be consuming. His new client was suing his job for sexual harassment.

Just the thought of his client's lawsuit sent Jonathan's mind racing. Men and women were finding the courage to come out and publicly accuse their harassers of assault. Even high ranking officials in public office had a slew of women accusing him of assault. No one was safe from harassment and it made Jonathan sad. He didn't understand how a country that had progressed so well in some areas, resembled the stone age in others.

Women were still fighting for their right to be heard in the boardrooms and offices around the globe. The lure of power pushed people to victimize and demean others. Harassment and assault were now hot topics in the news.

Sadly, folks still had trouble believing victims of assault. This prevented many from coming forward with their stories, allowing victimizers and harassers to go free. Jonathan witnessed first hand the level of vitriol that the public can spew towards a helpless victim.

Jonathan wondered if the cases were becoming more prevalent or if access to social media and the Internet exposed everything on a larger scale. No matter how he looked at it, the world was filled with an evilness that only God could heal.

It was so disconcerting for Jonathan. Jonathan said a silent prayer for clarity as he prepared for his next client, Carl Hickler.

Carl was a nurse at Lenox Hill Hospital where he complained that his supervisor, Marie Curtain made sexual advances towards him. Marie was the head nurse at Lenox Hill Hospital working in the NICU unit.

Marie appreciated her job but she loved the power that it brought to her. She wielded the power over every one of her staff members. Carl was the first who complained about the harassment, but he wasn't the first who experienced it.

After he refused her advances, Carl found himself in a precarious position. His supervisor purposed to make his life a living hell. She scheduled him for strange shifts that caused him to be on his feet for hours longer than he needed.

When he complained or expressed concern about his schedule she would conveniently suggest that he just quit. In fact, according to Carl she convinced the other nurses on the unit to ostracize him. He was left out of important meetings, his trainings were impeded and she was now after his performance reviews and professional standing at the hospital.

A negative performance review was used as the main reason behind his removal. He wasn't given a warning or an opportunity to address any of the negative assessments made against him.

A job that he once loved was the cause of his stress, heart palpitations and anxiety. Carl wanted to know if there was any recourse for his treatment at the hospital.

Jonathan had several clients to meet with in the morning and then he planned to head out of the office early. He needed a break.

If only he could have gotten an hour of sleep the previous night he wouldn't have been nearly as tired as he was. The nightmares were keeping him awake making him fearful of drifting off to sleep.

Instead he sat up in bed, questioning his next move. He knew what he had to do, he just didn't know how to explain it to Kelly. Jonathan's wife was understanding, she was his rock.

He made a decision to talk to her about his visions after dinner when the kids were settled and he could get her opinion without having to worry about interruptions.

Kelly would know exactly what he should do to ease his mind. She was the one who suggested that he return home when he experienced his first crisis last year. Although they weren't a religious family, Kelly often deferred to God's plan when they talked.

Jonathan took detailed notes as Carl poured his heart out to him while trying his hardest not to react to anything Carl was saying. Jonathan didn't intend on returning to his job after his situation in Jerusalem.

He expected to be changing careers from attorney to archeologist, but something happened to him while he was in that hole. His perspective on things changed.

After they stayed in Minnesota for a few extra days to assure his mother that he was completely fine, they returned to New York and continued on with their lives.

If it wasn't for the nightmares and the feeling of restlessness he wouldn't have thought that he had ever step foot inside Jerusalem. Was it all a dream? He knew the answer to that question. He felt every bump and bruise as his body tumbled down the hole at the excavation site. He remembered the feeling of his body hitting the ground *hard*.

He absently rubbed at the knot on the back of his head, his only reminder that the trip happened and wondered what his next step would be. There had to be a purpose for his pain, right?

Carl continued to talk about his experience at Lenox Hill Hospital as Jonathan struggled to stop his mind from wandering. By the time their meeting ended, Jonathan had formulated an amazing litigious plan for Carl that would get him justice.

His mind drifted to Living Waters Baptist Church, a bright morning with his grandfather standing at the pulpit preaching his heart out. He remembered a lot of his grandfather's sermons. Many of them were permanently etched in his mind.

He recalled the sermon about Jonah. Jonah wouldn't do what God instructed him to do out of fear. His disobedience to God's word ultimately caused him to run away from his home. He ended up being swallowed by a whale in order to serve his purpose.

Jonathan thought about the story that he had been told since he was a young child. Suddenly his office phone rang interrupting his thoughts. Reaching for the phone he smiled when the name came across the screen, Luke Flannigan was calling him right when he needed him the most.

"Hey Pop, how are you?" he asked sounding like the excited child that he became when he talked to his grandfather. Luke Flannigan was an integral part of his youth and adult life. He leaned on his grandfather and admired him so much that he knew when he heard his voice, that his grandfather would have the answer. Jonathan kicked himself for not involving his grandfather earlier, then sleep wouldn't have eluded him for so many nights.

"Hi son, I need to talk to you. Are you busy right now," his grandfather asked as if Jonathan would ever dismiss a call from his grandfather. "No sir, what's going on" he asked intrigued by his grandfather's mid day call.

Psalm 8: 1-2

"O Lord, our Lord, how great is Your name in all the earth. You have set Your shining-greatness above the heavens. [2] Out of the mouth of children and babies, You have built up strength because of those who hate You, and to quiet those who fight against You."

Chapter 9

She hummed along as the Butterfly Waltz began to play softly. The
audience began to clap as the little ladies made their appearance on the
Auditorium stage. This was their second competition of the year and the
girls were more excited about the event than anyone else in the
building.

Parents, grandparents and visitors crammed into the high school
auditorium to see their favorite gymnasts perform. At the conclusion of
the first performance, Jonathan greeted his daughters with a dozen
roses each. Watching how their eyes lit up with glee, she cried. Her
father wasn't as involved as Jonathan and it really was a lovely thing to
see how he interacted with them.

It was the cutest thing Kelly had ever witnessed.

The line of young ladies dressed in their pink and white leotards made
her smile. Kelly gave her husband's hand a loving squeeze when Brittany
pirouetted across the stage. Her green eyed gymnast completed her

floor routine, smiling brightly as she danced around the floor like the "Gabriella" song was made for her.

Her daughter's talent was clear and evident. Brianna danced around like the other girls, participating in the competition but not really there. Her eyes were all around the floor, but her sister danced about perfecting her turns and twists with supreme elegance.

"She's really good," Kelly heard a parent say behind her. "The cutie with the red bow is so adorable," they remarked as they gushed over Brittany. Kelly beamed with pride.

Kelly knew that her daughter possessed a great deal of talent. When Brittany begged her to sign up for the Paragon's Gymnastics Team, Kelly couldn't help herself. She was exploding on the inside with excitement. Being in the room watching her girls complete tumbling training she realized just how much fun she missed growing up.

Dance rehearsals, recitals and gymnastics were not a part of her childhood. Being the sixth child in a family of twelve, Kelly had to learn the fine art of sacrifice. She had no choice. Growing up in Hoboken, New Jersey wasn't the fairytale life that she promised her daughters would live.

In fact, she didn't have much of a childhood. She and her siblings worked odd jobs, bartended and did everything they could to bring extra money in the house.

Their father, Kyle Klein worked odd jobs here and there, but he never held down any position long enough to secure a comfortable life for his wife and children. Susan, her mother, was a different story. She worked tirelessly in the suburban homes of wealthy New York bankers and attorneys.

Susan was a domestic worker who provided for not only herself but her entire family. They resided in a home owned by Susan's parents. Susan was orphaned at the age of 16, her parents died in a car accident leaving her and her two siblings the house.

Kelly's mother raised her younger siblings and dropped out of school to provide for them. She had been sacrificing her entire life. It made Kelly sad to know that her mother spent her 72 years on the earth struggling and scraping to get by. She worked so hard that her children barely had a recollection of her doing anything besides leaving the house for work.

That was not the life she imagined for herself and her family. Kelly would break the curse of living paycheck to paycheck. She couldn't stand not knowing if there would be enough food for them to eat at night.

That was a life Kelly promised herself that her children would know nothing about. She worked hard and graduated high school. It wasn't an easy feat. Only three of her twelve siblings made it through high school. Kelly promised her mother that she would make something out of her life. "Do everything I didn't do, Kelly," her mother begged with pleading eyes as she watched her daughter leave New Jersey for the big city.

Security was something that Kelly sought from childhood. She knew what it was like to struggle for food, she didn't want to ever return to that. Kelly poured herself into her work. She waited tables, cleaned houses and attended college classes at Columbia in the evenings.

There wasn't much time for partying and relaxing or enjoying herself. She couldn't afford the luxury that some of her friends in high school had. They had parents who could afford to pay for their college education while they backpacked through Europe in the Summer and soaked in the Caribbean sun on spring break.

Kelly had a much harsher reality to face. She didn't have the privileges that her friends enjoyed and she knew better.

She was proud of where she came from and especially proud of the life she and Jonathan built for their daughters. Watching the look of peace on her daughter's face as she twirled on the stage looking like a flawless angel made her smile broadly.

She had made it.

She and her husband gave her girls a life that even she couldn't have imagined for herself. For that, she would be eternally grateful.

John 6:35

"Jesus said to them, "I am the Bread of Life. He who comes to Me will never be hungry. He who puts his trust in Me will never be thirsty."

Chapter 10

Luke Flannigan busied himself walking around the church inspecting everything before Wednesday evening Bible Study. The media ministry team were setting up the cameras and televisions to ensure that everyone in attendance had a clear view of the Bible verses that they intended to study for the evening.

Pastor Luke's most recent sermons were centered around the fruits of the spirit. He loved preaching about peace, joy, patience, charity, faith, modesty and self-control amongst others. There was something encouraging and motivating about the way God provided us with the things we really needed. Luke loved to remind his church family that peace, love and patience were things that they didn't have to petition to God. We didn't have to ask him for peace, it was a fruit of the spirit; a gift from God that didn't require any intervention on our own, besides faith.

Luke enjoyed the expressions of relief on the faces of his congregants when he preached about peace. "We already have peace in our hearts.

We need to activate our faith in God to access it. That's all it takes is your faith," he reminded his church on plenty of occasions. Luke also enjoyed the fact that he wasn't the only one teaching in the church. His congregants were the reason he remained abreast on technology.

He was still getting used to the technological advances that the church recently made. They were trying to bring the church into the new age and keep up with the changing technology landscape. His technology team were working on an Apple IOS app for his church parishioners. Pastor Luke wanted his church members to have access to their sermons at all times.

Services were already streamed online and he ministered to couples and the teen community through the podcast. Luke was determined to grow his church and to reach as many people as possible. He was aware of other Pastors who resisted technological change.

They preferred to keep their churches away from social media and technology. While he could respect that, Luke knew that his mission was greater than his comfort level. He fully immersed himself in all things technology to grow accustomed. He was proud that he now delivered his sermons from notes saved on his iPad.

God placed a sermon on Luke's heart that he planned to minister to his parishioners with, but there was a feeling tugging at his heart telling him that someone outside of the church desperately needed to hear his sermon more.

He loved his grandson, and although he didn't mention anything during their brief conversation earlier that morning, he knew that something was bothering him. Luke could hear the anguish in his grandson's voice. It was difficult to be a grandfather in his position.

Luke wanted to help Jonathan, but he wasn't sure how he could assist. He wanted to be there for him at all times, but he also understood that Jonathan was no longer a young impressionable child. He was now a grown man with a family.

Ministering to parishioners for over four decades taught Luke something. Just like Solomon wrote in the book of Ecclesiastes, there was a season for everything.

He understood that there was a time to speak and also a time to listen. Luke made sure that when he heard pain or fear in his loved one's voices, he need only to do one thing, listen.

Most people will tell you what is bothering them without having to say a word. Their voice, body language and demeanor says it all. He wished that he could be face-to-face with his grandson. He wanted to embrace him and let him know that everything would be alright.

Since he couldn't physically motivate his grandson, he took a deep breath and said a brief prayer for Jonathan and his family. He prayed for his grandson's strength but more importantly he prayed for Jonathan's ears and eyes were open to hear what the spirit of the Lord was trying to convey to him.

Luke felt strongly that he was to be alongside of Jonathan during the next chapter of his life. This placed a very heavy burden on Luke's heart but he was determined to be obedient to God and the will God had for his grandson's life.

Matthew 11:28-30

"Come to Me, all of you who work and have heavy loads. I will give you rest. [29] Follow My teachings and learn from Me. I am gentle and do not have pride. You will have rest for your souls."

Chapter 11

The lights and excitement on Broadway was bleak in comparison to the glee that filled Juniors, a cheesecake haven in Times Square. The girls feasted on slices of strawberry cheesecake that was much larger than both of their smiling faces as Jonathan and Kelly sipped on coffee and watched them both in silence.

Jonathan tried to stifle a yawn but it caught Kelly's attention. "You're still having trouble sleeping," she affirmed with a sad nod. "Do you want to talk about it," she asked as the girls played amongst themselves unaware of the conversation.

"I'm having strange dreams again," he confessed as she nodded understandingly. "I don't know how to interpret them," he continued as she listened intently. "Don't rush it. Meditate on it," she said as he smiled at her suggestion. "Maybe you should see Dr. Creek again," she said with a smile. Jonathan visited her weekly for a year trying to get a handle on the nightmares.

Now that the unsettling visions were back, he wondered if his wife was right. Maybe he should go see his therapist.

Kelly wasn't raised in a Christian household. She didn't know anything about prayer until Jonathan recently introduced it to her. When Jonathan returned from Jerusalem he had a new found sense of peace and purpose. He did a complete 180 degree turn on his wife and family. He went from being an Atheist to returning to his faith to the delight of his mother and grandfather he rededicated his life to Christ.

Jonathan worried about how his wife would take the news. When he returned to Minnesota his mind was already made up. He didn't try to change his wife's mind, she eventually began to understand his faith. Kelly enjoyed watching evangels on television. While she was intimidated by the entire church process, she loved listening to the preachers. She even followed several prominent preachers on Instagram for daily encouragement.

One program in particular caught her attention. The well dressed preacher spoke about spirit visions and how God speaks to us in dreams and through visions. That really piqued her interest. Kelly's interests in the Christian faith grew into a profound thirst for knowledge. This truly impressed Jonathan.

This was a treat for an amazing performance in the gymnastics competition. It was really just an excuse. Kelly and Jonathan had serious sweet tooth's and the girls definitely took after them. In fact, their first date was at the Juniors restaurant at Grand Central Terminal.

Kelly smiled as her mind drifted to their courtship. Her husband was her prince charming. She didn't let Jonathan meet her family. Her childhood wasn't something that she wanted to return to and sadly, visiting her family took her on a mental journey that she wasn't quite prepared for.

Her children had never met their grandparents. Jonathan didn't meet his in-laws and although he was close with his family, he never questioned her distance with her own relatives because he had become estranged from his own family. Kelly appreciated that. Jonathan was that type of person. He didn't like to discuss things that he felt would upset her.

He always wanted to see her smiling, so unless it was something important they didn't dredge up the past.

Once they finished their desserts they grabbed their jackets and headed towards the door. They were both exhausted and couldn't wait to return home so they could put an end to the late evening.

Psalm 34:10

"The young lions suffer want and hunger. But they who look for the Lord will not be without any good thing."

Chapter 12

Anna worked on her lesson plans while nibbling on a fruit salad in her bag. She was dedicated to her new fitness lifestyle and used fruit to satisfy her cravings for sweets. She was training for an upcoming half-marathon and she couldn't wait to cross the finish line. She could see and also taste the celebratory brownie sundae that she and her teammates had planned for after the run.

A knock on the door broke her concentration as she looked up at the source. Pastor Luke was standing in the doorway holding a large event poster, wearing a proud smile. "The poster finally made it," he exclaimed as she smiled in return. "That's wonderful! Just in time for the church's revival," she offered excitedly.

The Living Waters Baptist Church Annual Homecoming Event was one of the largest revivals in the state, drawing thousands to the church for celebrations and praise throughout the night. Hotels within a 25 mile radius were booked in preparation for the weekend event.

Pastor Luke invited a great deal of well-known Pastors, choirs and singing groups within the country. Everyone looked forward to the event, but no one was more excited than Luke Flannigan.

They had a carnival event planned for Saturday morning where Anna planned to bring her cousin's two children. She enjoyed her time with Kyle and Jordan. There was something magical about watching young children play and experience things for the first time. Deep down inside Anna longed to become a wife and mother.

She wanted to have two boys like her cousins' children and enjoy their laughter and zest for life with the man she loved. She knew that the dream was simply that; a dream but Anna also knew that God wasn't finished with blessing her.

She remembered the story in the Bible about Sara and how long she waited for a child. Although Anna wasn't keen on waiting nearly 100 years, she figured if Sara had the faith to wait that long for her blessing surely she could wait thirty years.

Instead of focusing on her romantic life, or the lack thereof, she poured herself into the church and activities at the school. Anna scheduled every minute of her life, making sure that she didn't have any time to reflect on just how lonely she really was.

In fact, Pastor Luke's presence in her office was a welcome distraction from her thoughts. She studied the poster, scanning it for errors or misspellings, just as any teacher is trained to do. Pastor Luke reviewed her PowerPoint slides for the children's event; marveling at the pictures on the screen.

"I can't believe they've grown so quickly," he said shaking his head in amazement. The end of the year program was always bitter sweet as the parents and teachers said farewell to the seniors and the students who they had grown to adore. Living Waters Baptist Church Annual Homecoming Event was also the largest event in their town. Residents who weren't regular church members flocked to the church grounds to enjoy the festivities and to fellowship.

Anna was on the planning team for the event and could feel the excitement growing as the time drew closer.

Isaiah 40:31

"But they that wait upon the LORD shall renew their strength; they shall mount up with wings as eagles; they shall run, and not be **weary**; and they shall walk, and not faint."

Chapter 13

Five days later, Jonathan found himself seated across from his beautiful doctor explaining to her how his dreams made him feel. The smell of cocoa emitting from the lit candle and the comfortable North African décor made the office feel like a safe haven. He never had trouble pouring out his heart in this office.

His psychiatrist was a petite black woman with the complexion of a Hershey's candy bar. She had fluffy natural hair that framed her lovely face and a bright, inviting smile. Her name was Dr. Yvonne Moody.

Her presence offered a sense of comfort that he was desperately grasping for. "What do you think your father is trying to tell you," she asks as he closed his eyes in reflection. "I don't know," he finally said throwing his hands in the air. "He wants me to do something," he said. "He kept saying that I need to..." he paused as he considered what he was saying.

He had to be careful. He didn't want to tell his doctor about his experience in Jerusalem. Instead of going into detail about the dream and the fall in the pit, he decided to give her the same sanitized version he offered his wife and mother. Jonathan didn't want to risk his doctor admitting him for hallucinations, but he realized that he was there for a reason.

The thought amused him and he chuckled to himself. He knew that he wasn't crazy. The experience was more than real, but he didn't want to let anyone in on that situation until he was able to fully process it all.

Jonathan felt ashamed about his situation. He couldn't confide fully in anyone without fear of looking like a lunatic. The issue became an internal battle for Jonathan because he wanted so desperately to have his life back. Jonathan longed to feel at peace again. He knew that the only way to get to the root of the issue was to discuss the full story, but he just couldn't do it.

After a long silence, his doctor spoke, "Jonathan, have you prayed about your dreams? Maybe God is trying to tell you something," she offered with a smile. Jonathan considered what she said with a smile and then began to open up about his thoughts.

"That's really what I think, but I don't know what I should be doing. I know that he wants me to warn the people about the visions I saw," Jonathan assumed allowed as his doctor watched him consider this thoughts.

"Maybe…I should Preach…I always wanted to do what my grandfather did. I wanted to be a Preacher but I didn't think that it would be something suited for me," he said looking down at his hands. "I think my dreams are telling me to preach the gospel to the world," Jonathan explained as he began to tell his doctor everything that happened to him in the pit.

Jonathan didn't go into full detail, but he told her everything that had been on his mind. Everything that kept him awake at night, he poured out to his doctor as she listened, intently.

Dr. Yvonne Moody listened to Jonathan speak. She watched his hands move around as he explained to her things he hadn't told anyone. She could feel his anguish and torment as he spoke. After considering her words for a while, she spoke.

"Jonathan, I think you need a break," Dr. Moody said. "I think you need to spend some time away from the office and regroup. I also think that you need to start spending more time in prayer. Quiet time and prayer time are quite beneficial to the mind, body and soul. Your grandfather is a Preacher? Speak to him about your visions. He will help you interpret things. You've got this, Jonathan," she encouraged with a smile.

An hour later Jonathan exited the office with a broad smile on his face. He knew exactly what he had to do to start his healing process.

Philippians 4:6-7

"Do not worry. Learn to pray about everything. Give thanks to God as you ask Him for what you need. [7] The peace of God is much greater than the human mind can understand. This peace will keep your hearts and minds through Christ Jesus."

Chapter 14

The summer vegetables were coming in rather nicely. It was late in the afternoon and she was outside enjoying the lovely day. She plucked the bright red, sun ripened tomatoes from the vine congratulating herself on another successful harvest.

Angela farmed for the enjoyment of it all. Since she lived alone she didn't have to worry about running out of fresh vegetables. Often times she brought large baskets of fruits and veggies to the church for parishioners to enjoy.

She had so many vegetables that she was propositioned by a local market to supply some of her fresh vegetables for sale at their outdoor stand. Angela wasn't interested, however. She farmed to help others not to sell to anyone.

The merchant owner, Mr. Dixon didn't understand her when she suggested that they give away the veggies to those in need.

Angela was raised as an only child and she didn't have a lot of friends growing up. She was a quiet, shy child but eventually found her voice when she met her husband Brad. He helped her become comfortable with herself. She blossomed with her husband and appreciated what he taught her about letting go of the inhibitions.

She was a very studious person, before Brad. Being a part of the Living Waters Baptist Church at a young age, Brad was already personable and well liked by the church congregation. When they started dating Angela feared the spotlight. She preferred to work with the children and the youth program. Brad wouldn't hear anything of it, though. He put Angela in front of the church congregation and let her shine.

Angela stepped outside of her shell because of her husband and spear headed the Little Ducklings Sunday School program which eventually grew into a fully accredited private school. Thanks to Angela, the school graduates nearly 40 students each year some with full International Baccalaureate degrees.

She marveled at the concept of parents and students clambering to attend the school. Angela couldn't believe that something she spearheaded could turn into an exclusive success.

She considered returning to the school to offer her help with the toddlers. They were her favorite little people in the church. Toddlers were so innocent and impressionable. They were little angels on earth and Angela enjoyed working with them most.

Angela made a note of contacting her father in law to see what he thought about her idea. He was careful about Angela over exerting herself in the ministry, but sometimes that lead to her feeling lonely. She decided that the next day she would contact Luke.

Standing from her kneeling position, she tried to balance herself on the stool in front of her, but suddenly lost her footing. Unable to catch herself from falling, she screamed in a panic. Angela fell backwards a violent snapping sound filled the air as she landed on her right arm. Screaming in shock, she immediately felt a searing pain run down her arm as she struggled to find the phone to call 911.

Psalm 4:8

"I will lie down and sleep in peace. O Lord, You alone keep me safe."

Chapter 15

Jonathan was finally resting in a state of complete relaxation, he was able to sleep peacefully for once. He figured that talking to his therapist and prayer both eased his mind to allow the invasion of sleep's peace. He decided to speak with his grandfather in the morning, like the therapist advised. Suddenly the vibrating sound next to his bedside made him sit up in fright.

Fumbling in the dark he grabbed his phone and answered it quickly. "Hello," he said groggily, while glancing at the clock. "Jonathan, this is Anna," the voice from the past sounded familiar, but odd. He saw Anna over a year ago and was gratified to see that she gave her life to God. It was reassuring to see how God can take our lives and make it new.

He remembered how encouraged her transformation made him feel. It gave him hope in his situation. Especially since Anna was taking care of his mother so well. It made Jonathan feel sterling to know that someone could turn their life around and come out looking as peaceful and happy as Anna did. Jonathan thanked her for taking care of his mother in his absence. She wouldn't hear of it.

Anna told Jonathan that it was the guidance of his mother that kept her on track. She thanked Jonathan for sharing his mother. They shared a great laugh and a tender moment that warmed everyone in the living room. That was nearly a year ago.

Jonathan would never forget how amazing that moment felt, having his mother, wife and old friend in the same place expressing nothing more than gratitude together. He didn't know what to make of her calling at 2:00 in the morning. "Your mother has been admitted to Regions Hospital. She broke her arm in three places," she gasped in a brittle voice.

Images of his mother in pain flashed through his mind and Jonathan couldn't help but think the worst. For the first time in a long time, he chastised himself for leaving Minnesota for New York City. It bothered him that he couldn't immediately be by his mother's side.

Instead of panicking, Jonathan took in a deep breath. He didn't want to upset Anna any further. She sounded more distraught than he felt. Jonathan could definitely understand Anna's anguish. Angela was a formidable force to be reckoned with. She rarely caught a cold without bouncing right back.

"How is she?," he asked, heart pounded out of his chest. Jonathan coughed as his throat suddenly felt like the Sahara desert. He reminded himself to react calmly so he didn't upset Anna. He could hear her crying softly on the phone as he gathered his thoughts.

"She's not doing well...She... fell in her.... garden and was there for over three hours before I arrived... I... couldn't get her on the phone," she said between sobs. "I finally just drove there and that's where I found her. She has a concussion... Jonathan," she said crying.

"A concussion?" he asked as her words continued to sink in. His mouth moved in a silent prayer as she continued talking. He thanked God for keeping his mother safe and for sending Anna to check on her. Anna was the closest person to Angela and he was blessed that she cared for his mother like she were her own.

Jonathan prayed as Anna spoke about Angela's condition, hoping to calm Anna and his own spirit before they ended their call. Jonathan didn't want to admit it, but he was terrified.

Although, Jonathan knew that God had full control of Angela's condition and He would protect her, he was still afraid of losing his mother. "God, please heal my mother. Please send Angels to stand charge around her bedside as I head to see her. Father God, I ask that you keep Anna comforted as she waits by my mother's bedside," he prayed as Anna continued rambling on the other end of the phone.

"I don't know what would have happened if I didn't get there," she said wailing, echoing his thoughts. "I can't believe that this happened to her. What will I do if something happens to her, Jonathan? Your mother has always been there for me. I don't have anyone else," she cried as Jonathan continued to pray.

At that moment Jonathan remembered that Anna and her mother didn't have the best relationship when they were younger. Angela stepped in the role of mother for so many people. Jonathan was used to hearing about the people she visited and cared for, thanking him for sharing his mother with them. Angela had the spirit of an angel. She was selfless and loving to everyone she encountered. Jonathan knew exactly how broken Anna felt, his heart ached with the same pain as he considered his mother's condition.

"Anna, take a deep breath," Jonathan instructed as she obliged. "I will be there as soon as I can catch a flight out there. Please don't panic. God has everything under control," he assured. Anna cried softly as Jonathan continued to speak. "Fear has no place in our hearts. We know who God is, we know what he can do, Anna," he consoled as her erratic breathing began to slow considerably.

Once Anna calmed down, he assured her that he was on the way and hung up the phone. Jonathan fell to his knees, crying out to God.

James 1:6

"You must have faith as you ask Him. You must not doubt. Anyone who doubts is like a wave which is pushed around by the sea."

Chapter 16

The flight to Minnesota from New York LaGuardia took nearly seven hours. By the time the plane landed Jonathan was so jetlagged that he knew for sure he wouldn't have trouble sleeping that night. All he wanted to do was see his mother.

He caught a taxi from the airport to the hospital, carrying his luggage in the car with him. Jonathan didn't want to spare any time. He couldn't get Anna's voice out of his mind. After she called him he informed Kelly who assured Jonathan that she would be fine with the girls in New York if he left on the redeye to Minnesota.

Jonathan was on a flight within three hours of Anna's phone call. He emailed Nancy and informed her that he would need two weeks of personal leave to make sure that his mother was safe.

When he arrived at the hospital he checked in at the reception area and asked for his mother's room. The walk to the ICU corridor felt like a ten mile trek. Jonathan was walking directly into the unknown. He wanted to run, but something told him that he needed to take his time. Anna didn't say that his mother was in the Intensive Care Unit of the hospital.

When he finally reached her room, he took in a deep breath and tried not to let a cry escape. She was in the room alone, lying in a small hospital bed. Jonathan gasped when he saw how small she appeared inside the bed. Angela was a fairly healthy person. She never spent any time inside of a hospital until that very moment. It shook Jonathan to his core to witness it all.

Angela had three different IV bags secured to her tiny frame. She was wrapped in blankets which made Jonathan smile. His mother was always cold, that's why she sipped tea so often. His mother was hooked up to a ventilator, she wasn't conscious and looked a lot worse than he expected.

For the first time in a long time, Jonathan felt helpless. He couldn't do anything to ease his mother's pain. He could tell by the bags connected to her IV that she was struggling with severe pain.

Jonathan didn't want to cry. He tried to hold himself together. He wanted to prove that he could be strong in the face of fear and he definitely was afraid. He couldn't lose his mother at that time. Jonathan depended on her comforting wisdom to get him through some difficult times.

He desperately needed her to heal.

Jonathan placed a gentle kiss on his mother's cheek and whispered to her, "I love you, Mom". He wanted to tell her how much seeing her in the bed like that terrified him. Jonathan wanted to confide in her that he couldn't imagine his life without her. He wanted to say a lot of things, but he couldn't. All he could do was rub her hand and plead with God to save his mother. He wondered if he should have stayed in Minnesota to take care of his mother instead of heading to New York.

His mother always said that she would love to have him, Kelly and the girls nearby.

The floodgates opened and he began to weep openly at the vision of his mother's helpless body in the bed. "Lord, please heal my mother. I ask that you leave ministering angels at my mother's bedside. Please bring her out of this with a testimony of your greatness," he declared as he closed his eyes tightly.

He could feel someone embrace him from behind. The familiar smell of Sandalwood and Spice wafted through his nostrils causing him to weep harder as his grandfather embraced him. "It's alright, son" he consoled. "We must have faith," Pastor Luke encouraged as Jonathan cried.

Pastor Luke placed a steady arm around his grandson's shoulders. Luke beamed with pride at what he just witnessed. His grandson prayed over his daughter in law in a pure and open hearted way. He admired the weeping young man that he helped raise.

"All is well, Jonathan," Luke encouraged. "God shows his hand in some of the most devastating situations," he reminded. Jonathan nodded his head in agreement. "I know," he said with a sad smile.

Pastor Luke thought about the situation and said a prayer of gratitude for his grandson. He was grateful that God softened Jonathan's heart. His grandson, the young man who he had to literally drag to church was now praying by his mother's bedside.

"God is good," Pastor Luke said. "Yes, he is," Jonathan added as they listened to the blood pressure machine take Angela's measurements. "Please save my mother," Jonathan whispered as his grandfather embraced him.

John 7:38

"The Holy Writings say that rivers of living water will flow from the heart of the one who puts his trust in Me."

Chapter 17

The bright sun beamed in through the floor to ceiling windows, shaking her awake. She barely slept the night before and she was even more exhausted today but there was no reason for her to lay in bed any longer. Her daughters had swim class downstairs in the pool room at noon and she also had an open house scheduled for four.

Kelly decided to bring the girls along with her to the open house showing. Brittany was a very good girl and she would keep her younger sister entertained while she showed the house on Central Park West. She couldn't wait to show Mr. Ting this last apartment. She truly saved the best for last.

It was this type of adrenaline that she felt when showing a house that gave her the feeling of complete satisfaction. She loved touring and showing new homes, making suggestions on improvements and getting the inside scoop on price adjustments. Kelly loved her job.

She quickly showered and dressed before getting the girls dressed for their swimming lessons. When they arrived at the pool she smiled at the sight of the eager preschoolers lining up for their chance to dive in.

Brittany tugged on her mother's sleeve. "Mom, can we go," she pleaded holding on to her sister's hand. The coach was just ahead waving them both towards her. Brittany squealed as her best friend, Gabriella called out her name and ran towards her.

An enchanting beauty with a bright smile, Gabriella was Brittany's best friend. Kelly adored their bond. They shared the same hobbies and passions. It was Gabriella who initially suggested that they try out for gymnastics. Her mother was an Olympic competitor in the sport years prior and she was grooming Gabriella to become her protégé.

It didn't take long to see that both girls were born gymnasts. Ever since her suggestion and coaching, there was no stopping Brittany. The girls practiced nonstop in an effort to perfect their routines. Gabriella and Brittany were quite creative and designed posters and drawings that Kelly proudly displayed around their home.

Suddenly, she was overcome by a coughing fit. She couldn't catch her breath as the wave of nausea and coughs consumed her tiny body. She shook violently as she tried to recover from the coughing fit. Kelly tried to gain her composure as helpless tears streaked down her red cheeks. She could feel the eyes of everyone in there on her, wondering what was wrong with her.

Kelly couldn't blame them for gawking, she was wondering the same thing. Her allergies were driving her crazy. It had to be something in the air because this was the second coughing fit she'd had in a matter of days.

Some sweet soul brought her a bottle of water to try and calm the coughing fit. As she struggled to catch her breath, she took a seat on the white plastic pool chair with a dark blue stripe across the middle. She sat in the chair for much longer than she expected.

One of the mothers in Brianna's daycare came running to her aide. "Kelly, relax for a while," she insisted when Kelly tried to jump up too quickly. "I'll make sure that the girls are fine. They're in Skylar's class anyway," she offered as Kelly opened her mouth to protest.

Skylar's mother waved an impatient hand in front of Kelly. "I will hear nothing else about it. Please just sit here for a minute. I understand how it is. Us mothers have to stick together," she joked as they laughed together.

Kelly felt horrible about sharing her responsibilities, especially burdening someone else with her children, but she desperately needed the help. If it wasn't for her afternoon showing she would lay in bed for the rest of the day.

She was exhausted.

Kelly wondered if she was pregnant. The last time she felt this way she was three months pregnant with Brianna. Her heart rate quickened with fear and adrenaline. She wasn't expecting to have more than two children. In fact, she would have been a happy mother of one child if God saw fit. Coming from a large family, she didn't see any benefit in having more mouths to feed than necessary.

Fighting siblings for a seat at the dinner table for meager rations. It wasn't a terrible childhood but definitely not one that she wanted to repeat for her kids. She found herself sharing much too often, as a young child and Kelly didn't want her children to have to sacrifice as much as she did.

She also witnessed her mother have children until she couldn't any longer, then she spent her life dedicating herself to giving them the best she possibly could. A very limited education and more responsibilities than help, her mother didn't live a long happy life.

It was a noble and honorable thing, but Kelly didn't want to have to do that. She and her husband decided that two children was the magic number for them. She considered her husband's stress levels, especially with his mother in the hospital.

Suddenly, the thought made her smile. A baby might be just what they needed to bring more joy to their family. With his mother being ill, maybe a baby would be a welcomed distraction. She then considered her career and thought, "maybe not".

Could they really handle another baby at this time?

1 Thessalonians 5:16-18

"Rejoice always, [17] pray without ceasing, [18] give thanks in all circumstances; for this is the will of God in Christ Jesus for you."

Chapter 18

"That was a pretty powerful prayer you said over your mother, son," Luke said as he watched Jonathan's face for a reaction. Jonathan's face remained neutral as he considered his grandfather's words. It was strange that he felt compelled to pray for his mother in such a way. He was just rededicating himself to the gospel. Even though he did it before, when he was in dire trouble, it felt strange for him to call on the name of Jesus in such a way.

Jonathan didn't say anything to his grandfather but he was feeling more and more compelled to study the word of God. He didn't want his grandfather to get his hopes up too high. The old man would have him standing in front of the church preaching a sermon if he knew what was on Jonathan's mind.

"Well, you came just in time for the revival festivities. I'm sorry it was under these circumstances," he said blowing on the cup of dark liquid that he grasped between his hands. They were seated in the hospital food court talking over some of the strongest coffee he'd ever tasted. After they shared a laugh about the strong brew, they continued talking about Angela's fate.

"When Anna called, I didn't expect any of this," he said waving his hands high in the air to show the magnitude of what he was referring too. "Yes, son I didn't want you to know the dire situation that your mother was in. She fell pretty hard. The doctors initially thought that she suffered from a stroke but thankfully, the bleeding was caused by the fall. They were able to stop it, but the swelling is still pretty severe," he said sadly. "I helped pour that concrete slab," he said shaking his head in frustration. "She fell and hit her head on that slab and that's why she's in there," he said frustrated as Jonathan shook his head.

"God is in control," he assured his grandfather. "Everything happens for a reason. Mom will be fine. You need to get home and get some rest, Pop," he said as his grandfather yawned. "I'm fine," he said as they both laughed. "They expect your mother to remain in the medically induced coma for two days and they will gently bring her out," he reassured.

"I'm just glad that Anna was there," Jonathan declared with a sad smile. "Me too. I was at the church when she called me in hysterics. Poor Anna has grown quite close to your mother over the years. She leans on your mother," Pastor Luke offered.

During her teenage years Anna was a bit of a rebel. She and Jonathan were great friends but her destructive habits began to negatively affect them both. Drugs, promiscuity and pain were a large part of Anna's past, until she found the strength to pull herself out of the destructive pit. That's where Angela stepped in and helped Anna complete her journey towards redemption and sobriety. Unlike so many others who judged Anna's situation and turned her away, Angela saw the person behind the pain.

"That's why blessing others will bless you. If your mother turned Anna away like everyone else did, she wouldn't have someone who cared about her enough to physically go and check on her when she didn't answer the telephone. Anna has blessed our family," he said just as Anna walked into the cafeteria.

"Speak of the devil," he said jokingly as Anna walked towards the table. "How are you, Anna," Jonathan asked as he embraced his longtime friend. "I'm hanging in there. The doctors say that your mother is doing better. She's a fighter, but we all knew that," she said wearing a reassuring smile.

"I'm heading home to shower and rest for a bit. I will be back in the morning to check on your mother. I'm believing God for a miracle. I believe that your mother will be out of her coma tomorrow instead of two days from now," she said embracing both men again.

"Take care," she said heading towards the exit of the building. "Anna wait," Jonathan called after her as he caught up with her in the long marbled corridor. Doctors, nurses and visitors navigated around them as they tried to find somewhere quiet to talk.

Jonathan noticed how guarded Anna appeared. Gone was the fun loving girl with the cigarette hanging out of her mouth and a bottle of brew in her hand. She was replaced by a kind, gentle, timid spirit. Jonathan was amazed by the transformation. God truly could make all things new. He prayed that his transformation would be just as powerful.

"I just want to thank you for being there for my mother, for calling me and for being such a great friend," he said as he watched Anna's face crumble while she sobbed.

He held Anna tight. "It's gonna be okay, Anna," he said as he began to say a prayer of peace over Anna. This was the third time today that he had literally laid hands on someone and prayed. Jonathan was beginning to scare himself. The fact that his prayers were instinctive and not a reactionary or requested thing confused and concerned him.

"I'm acting like my grandfather," he said chuckling as he walked back towards the table. When he reached the table his grandfather didn't say a word, he simply nodded his head in understanding.

Jonathan gave Pastor Luke a pat on his back and nodded as they bowed their heads and prayed for Angela.

1 Peter 3:15

"But sanctify the Lord God in your hearts: and be ready always to give an answer to every man that asketh you a reason of the hope that is in you with meekness and fear."

Chapter 19

The applause in the building was deafening. Jonathan's heart leapt as he sat in the front row of the church facing his grandfather. It felt like old times again. The décor had been updated. The old projector and screen that he remembered so fondly were replaced with brand new LCD screens and a full sound system ensured that Luke's booming voice was heard throughout the building.

He was delighted to see some of the same parishioners sitting in their favorite spots, just as he remembered as a young child. The energy he felt from sitting in the church as the praises filled the building was literally indescribable. Jonathan yearned for this feeling again.

Jonathan's heart felt at peace. It was a feeling that had eluded him for decades, but at that very moment standing in the church he felt a strange yet resolving sensation. He felt at home.

He worshipped and praised with the rest of the congregation, finally letting go of himself after years of skepticism. Watching his grandfather lead the choir in a new rendition of, "He's Sweet I Know," Jonathan swayed with the music and allowed his mind to relax, for once. He took in a deep breath as he stilled his racing thoughts. He didn't want to ask for anything, he simply wanted to praise God for saving his mother's life.

Angela was out of the Intensive Care Unit and in the care of a full time nurse at her home. Jonathan wouldn't have had it any other way. His mother wouldn't have either. In fact, she insisted.

Even though she wasn't mobile, she was unrelenting. She demanded that they get her out of the hospital as soon as possible. Jonathan obliged her request. He hated the fact that she had to be confined in the depressing, sterile environment. Angela needed the familiarity of her home to heal properly.

He didn't care where she wanted to stay, Jonathan was just happy that his mother was out of the hospital. He gave up his hotel room and decided to stay with his mother. Although the strong and courageous Angela Flannigan, initially refused he finally talked her into letting a nurse visit her to check in on her while he was in New York.

He took a leave of absence from his job to take care of his mother. He didn't plan to return for two months thanks to the Family Medical Leave Act (FMLA) he wasn't concerned about losing his job while he cared for Angela. He felt blessed to be able to take care of his mother and return to a job afterwards.

Jonathan felt torn. He wanted to be by his wife's side every moment. He had fun with Kelly. They were best friends and they enjoyed their adventure of having two little girls. He just didn't feel comfortable leaving his mother. She looked much better than she did in the hospital but he still felt cautious for her.

Kelly assured him that she was doing fine without him. She told him that she missed him desperately, but the girls were keeping her so busy that she didn't have time to think about it much. He planned to fly home within the next week. He just wanted to be sure that his mother had all of her help in place before he left town.

She was a strong woman.

He wanted to talk to Anna about staying with his mother when he left for New York, but didn't know how to approach the subject with her. He closed his eyes and prayed for the courage to ask her and then he prayed for God to soften Anna's heart to the possibility.

As the spirit of God flowed through the building he felt the tension in his mind subside.

He finally found his place of peace.

"Well, I'm sure everyone has heard about the most recent church shooting that occurred on Thursday," he said pausing solemnly as the church congregants nodded sadly. "We are living in troublesome times, when someone can enter a place of worship and open fire. Folks are deliberately burning churches and mosques! Violence and hate have consumed the world, but fear not, God reminds us that He has overcome the world," Pastor Luke added to a roar of applause.

As he surveyed the congregation, he smiled at the now optimistic looking faces. "I want everyone to continue to pray for the Church of Notre Dame in Paris," Pastor Luke continued speaking as he glanced out into the congregation. His eyes searched the room looking for the Living Waters Baptist Church Community Director, Brenda Johnson. "Sister Johnson, please raise your hand," he requested as she waved proudly. "If you have any donations to send to the Church of Notre Dame, please see Sister Johnson after service," he advised.

"I would like to open the floor up for testimony," Luke offered once the music began to settle down. Hands shot up across the church with people presenting their powerful life testimonies one by one. Jonathan listened to each testimony with quiet gratitude.

God had delivered so many people from destruction. He knew that he wasn't the only person that God delivered but hearing the personal stories of being on the streets and God placing someone in their lives to help them find housing to the compelling stories of parents with children in prison. Each story exposed another facet of the love that God had for his people.

Jonathan was grateful for his life. He felt compelled to give a testimony on how God saved his life. He didn't know how he would do it, though. Jonathan was a shy person, he wasn't one for the spotlight.

Suddenly, he heard his name being called. Turning his attention to the front of the church he noticed his grandfather looking him in the eye. "Jonathan would you like to say a few words," he asked offering his grandson the microphone.

Jonathan was in awe. His grandfather never did this before. Why was he doing it now? Could he tell that Jonathan yearned to share his testimony?

Standing slowly, Jonathan nodded as the entire congregation erupted in applause. When he made it to the pulpit, the congregation was silent curiously awaiting his testimony. "How many of you know that Jesus is a healer?" he asked as multiple "Amen" echoed throughout the building.

"God saved me from a pit of destruction. I was at the worst point in my life and God pulled me out of it," he said. "I realized that rock bottom had a basement level, that's where Jesus met me," he said looking around the large building. Everyone was waiting for his next word. Jonathan couldn't wait to encourage people with his experiences.

He wanted them all to know that God was a healer, a deliverer and he would never let them down. As he talked to the congregation he also ministered to himself.

"He came down to me because he knew that I had no way of climbing up. I couldn't crawl up, all I could do was wait on him and I'm so glad that I did," he said as members of the church continued to shout, "Amen!" in response to his words.

Jonathan talked about his testimony. He told the congregation how he was delivered from a life of unsavory living. How he was an unbeliever heading straight to destruction and God stopped the cycle. He brought him out.

"You know you're favored when not only does he save you, he saved your friends too," he said thinking about Anna. "I come to you today to say, if you find yourself searching for your purpose simply do this," he said placing his hand over his chest. "This pounding, this beating drum is your indicator of purpose. As long as you have a heart beating in your chest, you have an assignment in the kingdom," he said as everyone in the building stood to their feet, clapping.

Several members stood to their feet and waved their hands towards Jonathan, encouraging him to continue to speak the truth. Jonathan continued to confess his sins, he talked about everything that God delivered him from. He shared that he used to drown his sorrows in alcohol and fast women. Some members who remembered him as a child gasped at Jonathan in awe. He could read the looks on their faces. No one expected Jonathan to be hard headed, to do the things he confessed to during his testimony. A week ago he wouldn't have considered sharing his story, but suddenly he was pumped with adrenaline. He wanted the world to know how God saved his life.

After he shared the truth about his past, who he used to be; he talked about that night in the cave. He talked about how God saved his life. He didn't share everything that happened in the cave, that would forever remain a secret. He shared enough to encourage the church members and let them know that God was a healer, a deliverer but most importantly, he was patient.

Their applause brought tears to his eyes as he turned to face his grandfather. Luke had a look of pure pride on his face. Jonathan hadn't seen that look since his father was alive. His heart leapt for joy. He recalled the story of Moses who fled from Egypt and wandered in the desert for many years before God called him to his purpose.

He found his purpose.

Hebrews 6:10

"For God is not unrighteous to forget your work and labour of love, which ye have shewed toward his name, in that ye have ministered to the saints, and do minister."

Chapter 20

"I love you more," Kelly said breathlessly in the phone. She missed her husband and couldn't wait until he returned. Not only was she lonely, Kelly was exhausted. Between work, home and her relentless pursuit of happiness she truly was out tasked. She wanted to fulfill all of her obligations, but she knew that she was burning the candle at both ends.

Being a mother was a full time job and her positions as both wife and realtor both demanded her full attention. Many nights she lay awake worrying, plotting and planning her next move. Her husband thought that she was fast asleep but she couldn't sleep.

How could she sleep when Mr. Ting was planning to make his final decision on which home he would purchase in the morning? She had to get Brittany and Brianna to the daycare fully dressed for their school program. Every night, it was like a running tape, playing in the back of her mind, nagging at her senses.

Kelly wanted a break, but who was she going to ask for reprieve? Jonathan was out in the Midwest taking care of his mom and she didn't live near any family. Even if she did she wouldn't imagine contacting any of them or place her children in their care.

What was a woman to do?

Exhaustion was behind her clumsiness. She was sure of it. After a dizzy spell caused her to lose her balance walking down the hallway of their apartment complex, she broke down and decided to schedule an appointment with her primary care physician. The bruise she sustained from the fall served as an urgent reminder to reduce the stress and get some sleep.

She and Jonathan were careful, but if she were pregnant again she would just chalk it up to being a part of God's plan for her life. Although, she wanted to expand the Real Estate firm and couldn't fathom setting her goals aside, she knew that her plans were not as important as her family. Kelly figured that she would be able to expand the business a few months after the baby started daycare. She chuckled at the old saying, "God laughs at your plans".

Maybe she would have a boy this time or another brilliant girl would be a blessing too. She toyed with the idea of being pregnant again. She would work until her last trimester, just as she did with her previous pregnancies. Even though, this pregnancy was getting off to a rough start. She was already tired before her second trimester.

She didn't tell Jonathan about her suspicions. Kelly figured if she could get a doctors appointment in time she would meet Jonathan with the ultrasound photo and all of the information at the airport. The surprise would be a welcomed one. They both love children and wouldn't mind the addition.

Kelly busied herself writing down ideas on the notepad next to her bedside. She was growing excited about a fourth addition to the Flannigan family. Ari was the name she wrote on the notepad paper. Seeing her baby's name written on the paper made it all the more real.

"In three days we will know for sure," she said anticipating the positive pregnancy test with a smile.

2 Corinthians 5:20

"Now then we are ambassadors for Christ, as though God did beseech you by us: we pray you in Christ's stead, be ye reconciled to God."

Chapter 21

Jonathan hung up the phone with Kelly still feeling the excitement coursing through his veins. He was on a natural, spiritual high. After being in the pulpit and sharing his testimony he felt compelled to do it again. There was something healing about having the ability to tell other people where God brought him from.

Jonathan also felt a deep desire to warn the world of the torment they would face if there were no God. The visions that flashed through Jonathan's mind when he was down in the pit haunted him. At night he suffered from horrible nightmares of what would happen if there were no God. He knew that God revealed it all to him on purpose. He had a duty.

Jonathan had to share with people how terrible the world would become if God was removed from their hearts and minds.

He told the story. Not the full story, but he told his story. He could see his mother sitting in the front row, tears streaming down her cheeks as she listened to her son encourage hundreds of people just like his grandfather.

The entire experience was life changing for him. He already made up his mind what he was going to do next. If his wife agreed with him then he was heading into a completely different dimension in his life and he couldn't wait to begin.

Lost in his thoughts, he didn't notice his mother sitting across from him at the table sipping warm tea. She studied him for a while before finally clearing her throat to speak.

"How are Kelly and the girls doing?" Angela asked Jonathan as he hung up the phone and sat down beside her on the couch. "They're doing well. Gymnastics, dance class and ballet. They're keeping Kelly busy. I miss them," he said sighing as she smiled. "I know you do. I'm grateful that you are here with me. I'm feeling better now son. The doctor has cleared me to be home alone, resting. It's time that you cleared me," she joked lovingly as they shared a laugh.

"Mom," he asked as she continued to play with the lemon in her tea absently. "Yes, son," she waited patiently.

"I'm thinking about joining the ministry," he blurted out with his eyes closed tightly as she nodded in agreement. Confused by the silence,

Jonathan opened his eyes and watched as his mother continued sipping her tea as if he didn't just drop a bombshell on her.

"Mom did you hear me," he asked thinking that she had to be losing her hearing if she didn't respond to what he just told her. He expected her to laugh, scream, yell or cry. He expected some type of reaction from her. Instead she watched him intently.

"Watching you up there today was enlightening Jonathan. You had a light surrounding you as you lead and encouraged through your testimony. I support your decision," she said as he embraced her.

"You already knew what I was going to say, didn't you," he asked as she nodded. "I'm a mother, Jonathan. I know everything," she said sipping her tea while he laughed at her thanking God for blessing him with Angela for a mother.

He couldn't wait to get on the plane and tell his wife the good news. It was settled. He was going to do something that would make God proud. Jonathan didn't know how to start and he didn't know what to do with his decision. Would he leave his job? Would he preach in New York? He wondered a lot of things that night as he lay in bed alone meditating on the days events.

It didn't take him long to decide that no matter what he did, next, he knew that he would be using his light to bring people to the ministry. He would be sharing his testimony with the world.

After he made his decision, he closed his eyes and slept peacefully through the night knowing that he was finally fulfilling his purpose.

Psalm 119:30

"I have chosen the way of truth: thy judgments have I laid before me."

Chapter 22

Luke Flannigan unlocked the doors to his modest sized brick home and chuckled to himself, recalling the prayer that his grandson spoke over the congregation just after he completed his testimony. His grandson spoke with such wisdom and grace. The members of the church couldn't wait to speak with him after service.

Elder Stanton and Brother James were two members within the Living Waters Baptist Church's Council. They along with two members from the treasury department and his church secretary worked as a team to run the church and schools smoothly.

"Pastor, did you hear Jonathan?" Brother James questioned with a broad smile. "I think he may be the next Flannigan to lead this church," he said with a note of pride. Elder Stanton pointed at the picture hanging on Pastor Luke's wall and cleared his throat. "Your father would be so proud of how his great grandson moved the congregation today," he said with a reassuring pat on Luke's back.

It was as if he could read Luke's mind. Watching his grandson give his testimony was bittersweet for Pastor Luke. He had visions of his son preaching and taking over the reins at Living Waters. When Brad died, he figured all was lost, but now. What if Jonathan chose to continue the family legacy of preaching the word of God?

It made Luke feel proud.

Once he settled in a pair of University of Minnesota sweats and an old t-shirt he turned the television on and settled on the couch to watch the nature channel. His cell phone buzzed alerting him to a message. He didn't have to look at the message to tell that it was Shawn from the media team.

He wanted to let him know that the video for the service was available online. Pastor Luke Flannigan couldn't wait to see the video again. He could only imagine how he stared on in amazement as Jonathan's testimony moved the congregation to tears.

He was astonished to see that altar call drew more people than he had seen in a while. His grandson's testimony was leading people to Christ and that was an amazing thing.

Luke considered the possibility of his grandson being called to preach and wondered if Jonathan felt the calling the way he had. Luke was only a teenager when God placed it in his heart to follow him. He never looked back and never regretted a moment of it.

Some of his friends decided that his way of living wasn't for them, but that was perfectly fine for Luke. He knew that the calling on his life would sustain him and it did.

He met his beautiful wife and had a family that he could've only imagined in his dreams. Luke was blessed to follow God's lead and he hoped that his grandson would see it the same way. He had friends in the ministry who struggled with their purpose for years, some for decades, but somehow they managed to find their way back home.

He knew that either way, Jonathan would find his way back to the Lord. Luke just didn't expect it to be that way. He knew that his grandson experienced something life changing in Jerusalem. He too experienced something that he would never forget. Although, he heard Jonathan tell him how he dreamed of a world with no God, hearing him tell everyone in the congregation moved him.

At the time, when Jonathan first told the story he dismissed Jonathan's visions as hallucinations. Robert Wellington explained everything to him and he didn't have to hear it from Jonathan to know that he survived an ordeal. Hearing about the hours that he spent in the sinkhole, in darkness; alone. It broke his heart.

He was so concerned about Jonathan's safety that he didn't really listen to the story. He heard Jonathan and he listened, but he didn't open his heart to really *listen*. Hearing it from Jonathan with such detail made his heart pound heavily in his chest. The story sounded so real, it was vivid.

Jonathan spoke of preachers being persecuted in the streets just for preaching the word of God. He talked about people turning their backs on the church, turning their backs on God.

He talked about how it all made him want to end his own life and that really hit Luke hard. Suicide was a near and dear subject to Luke. He lost a young parishioner to suicide four years ago and ever since he implemented suicide prevention classes and trainings to get everyone on board with recognizing the signs of severe distress.

Jonathan said that in his dream the suicide rates increased and it wasn't adults, but sadly the rise was in the middle to high school age groups. Babies who hadn't begun to live were making permanent choices like that. It was so upsetting that people wept openly in the service, but then he noticed the expressions change when Jonathan talked about his redemption story. How he was able to relax and let God soften his heart to heed his word.

He held the entire audience captive as he passionately expressed how he felt like the prodigal son, returning to Christ after all of those years being an Atheist. How he begged God to let him come home after years of denying his presence he found himself pleading for his assistance.

The most important thing about the entire testimony was the fact that he gave all honor and glory to God, not to himself for being saved from the pit. He didn't want to anyone to walk away from their seats with the notion that he did it on his own.

Jonathan proclaimed with his hands held high in the air and tears streaming down his cheeks, "look at what God has done for me," as the building erupted in praise to God.

Luke didn't tell his grandson at that moment but he knew that he had a calling on his life. He was going to preach the word of God to the masses and Luke prayed that he would be right there by his grandson's side to keep him encouraged.

2 Timothy 4:5

"But watch thou in all things, endure afflictions, do the work of an evangelist, make full proof of thy ministry."

Chapter 23

Jonathan exhaled loudly as he collapsed in the soft leather chair inside his mother's brightly decorated den. "What's wrong, Jonathan?" Angela questioned. Jonathan didn't have a response for his mother. He stared blankly at the canary yellow paint on the wall behind Angela. "I know what I have been called to do and I really want to do well, Mom," he said as Angela nodded in agreement.

"Mom, there are fifteen churches in the Arrowhead township, alone. Not one of them have invited me out to minister to their people. I'm getting so discouraged. I spent money on a publicist to try and get the word out so I could spread the gospel and nothing is panning out how I intended," he said as his mother listened to him vent.

Angela didn't say a word. She just let her son speak. Her listening skills improved as Jonathan aged. She was able to let go of the reins enough to listen to him without the urge to offer advise, unless requested, of course.

"I was fired up and ready to do this in the beginning. Now, I'm wondering if this is my path. Does that make sense?," he asked looking at her with pleading eyes. "Son, remember the story of Paul in the Bible. He was a fierce fighter of the gospel and then later found himself preaching the same gospel that he despised to others. He faced a great deal of ridicule, pain and frustrations as well, but he had a mission. He knew that what he was tasked to do was greater than his comforts," Angela reminded as her son wiped away a helpless tear.

Shaking her head sadly Angela stood and placed her right hand on her son's forehead. She closed her eyes and began to pray. "Dear God, we come to you today with gratitude in our hearts and minds. We thank you for the gifts that you have placed within Jonathan and for the direction that you provide. I ask that you speak to Jonathan. Help him understand that the path he's on may not be a comfortable one, but it has a purpose in your Kingdom. Please give him comfort and understanding, Father God. In Jesus Name I pray," she said as they both ended the prayer with a tearful, "Amen" Angela embraced her son.

It hurt her deeply to see Jonathan in this condition, especially when there was nothing that she could do to ease his frustrations. Angela watched as Jonathan's enthusiasm for sharing his testimony waned. She tried to keep him encouraged, but it wasn't an easy task.

It was painful for Angela to witness her son's discouraged demeanor, but she knew that even Jonathan's frustration served a purpose. "Have your way, God," she whispered.

Several days later, Jonathan received his final rejection notification from Saint Michael Church. It hurt Angela to watch him as he prepared himself to leave Minnesota. Angela could tell that his situation weighed heavily on his mind.

Angela held on to her son for dear life as he prepared to leave his childhood home. She handed him a small knapsack with homemade granola and snacks for the trip. They both shared a laugh at his sack lunch. Jonathan held his mother's hands in his own. "Mom, please take care of yourself," he begged as she nodded her response. "Of course, son. I have been thinking about doing something different, especially now that I can move around with more ease," she said spinning in a circle as they laughed together.

"Don't get too carried away," Jonathan teased. When Angela closed the door behind Jonathan she thanked God for healing. It felt good to be up and moving around. She was feeling more energetic and happy that progress was happening.

She was determined not to lye down in despair and waste away. She had too much to do with her life. While she rested in the hospital for that week after her fall she imagined a different life for herself. One where she remained dedicated to helping in the church but where her life expanded to traveling and experiencing things outside of her home.

What was the point in being alive and surviving her ordeal if she was going to crawl back on the couch and mope about her life not being full. She was going to create a full life for herself.

She watched as Jonathan's taxi headed out of the long driveway towards the airport. She missed her son already, but that didn't matter at the moment. She was more worried about her next project, Phase III of her life.

Angela felt like Phase I was becoming an adult and securing a future for herself, getting married and starting a family. Phase II in her life involved raising her son to adulthood. Phase III was all about Angela having fun and living blissfully.

She opened the newspaper and flipped through the paper to the Community section. She suddenly felt a rush of happiness as she read the course description for her first class. Abstract Art 101. It seemed fun enough and she always wanted to create visual art using paint.

"This is going to be super fun," she declared as she filled out the enclosed registration form and ripped it out of the newspaper. She smiled to herself as she tucked the paper inside her wallet.

This class was going to change her entire life.

Isaiah 40:29

"He giveth power to the faint; and to them that have no might he increaseth strength."

Chapter 24

For the first time in weeks Kelly awoke with strength and vigor in her step. She couldn't have been happier. Jonathan was back home resting peacefully and they both slept well through the night. She was happy that things had worked themselves out.

She was taking the day off to visit the doctor and to pamper herself. Kelly needed to rejuvenate and replenish so she scheduled herself a massage and mani/pedi at the Robert Andrews Spa. She couldn't wait to relax in the spa chair.

First she had a doctors appointment to get out of the way. She didn't tell Jonathan about the appointment. She wanted to come home and surprise him with the news about the new baby. She was convinced by this point that she was pregnant.

Glancing at the calendar and thinking back to her cycle she figured that she was only a few weeks pregnant. That gave them plenty of time to secure a new place to live.

She loved their current apartment but it was just enough for three people, four would definitely be a crowd. Especially since babies required so much more things than anyone else.

She had her eye on one of the complexes that she showed Mr. Ting earlier in the week. She figured if they were aggressive they could be moving into their new place before she started showing. The thought made her smile as she swung open the glass door to enter her doctor's office suite.

Kelly sat down in the waiting area and flipped through the maternity magazine thinking back to five years ago when she was pregnant with Brianna. It was a wonderful time. She enjoyed both of her pregnancies. Having a little life growing inside of her was a humbling experience that she welcomed again.

When the nurse called her name she smiled brightly and headed inside the lab to have her weight and blood pressure checked. The slim brunette nurse had a warm smile with thin lips and sincere eyes. She glanced down at Kelly's chart, "you've lost ten pounds since your last visit. I would love to know what diet you've been on," she joked as Kelly considered her words.

She was losing weight.

"Have you had any issues or questions lately that you would like to share with Dr. Comberbach," she asked as Kelly nodded. "Insomnia," she said as the nurse nodded. "Don't we all," she remarked escorting her to the office.

Kelly looked around the white sterile looking office and shivered. Aside from the posters hanging on the wall, she didn't see any warmth in the room, but that was how doctor's offices were to her, cold and empty.

Her visit brightened the moment her doctor walked into her office. Dr. Cumberbach was a sweet woman with a sassy hair cut and a zest for life. Her vibrancy was the main reason why Kelly chose her as her physician. Dr. Cumberbach lit up any room that she entered.

"So, Kelly it's been a while. What brings you in?" she asked after embracing Kelly and exchanging pleasantries.

"I haven't been feeling like myself lately," Kelly began talking as her doctor flipped through her notepad reading her vitals, no doubt. "I've been exhausted and having dizzy spells" she said as her doctor gently placed the clipboard on the white sterile countertop and touched the sides of Kelly's neck with her two fingers.

She pressed softly and continued examining Kelly as she encouraged her to continue to voice her health concerns. She completed the exam by shining a tiny light in Kelly's bright eyes and letting out an exhaustive sigh.

"I think I might be pregnant," Kelly blurted out with a smile as her doctor nodded. "Well, we can certainly do some blood work to be sure, but I also want to do a routine screening to be on the safe side," she offered.

"It shouldn't take any longer than a day or so to get the results. I'll have my office call you once the results are in," she said standing and offering Kelly a hug of reassurance as she left the room.

"Don't worry, Kelly. God has everything under control," she assured as Kelly relaxed. She also chose her doctor because she was a Christian. Her doctor was more of a believer than Kelly but she wanted to be close to someone spiritual, someone who believed that there was someone bigger than them.

2 Thessalonians 3:3

"But the Lord is faithful, who shall stablish you, and keep you from evil."

Chapter 25

They sat at the dinner table munching on flatbread pizza and salad as the kids played. They made up another song which they were trying out on their captive audience. Kelly was tired but she felt great about her doctors appointment. In a few days she would have her confirmation to what she already knew to be true.

She reached across the table and gave Jonathan's hand a tight squeeze. He was bubbling with excitement and couldn't wait to complete their dinner. Jonathan walked in the house earlier that day and announced that he had something that he wanted to discuss with her.

They were planning on heading to Juniors to share a dessert and to have a moment to talk after dinner. Kelly arranged to have a babysitter come over to watch the girls while they talked. She enjoyed that aspect of their relationship. They still dated each other. That was one of Kelly's marriage requirements when she and Jonathan started dating.

He took her to places that she couldn't have imagined enjoying. They spent afternoons reading poetry in the massive New York Public Library. They challenged each other to pool games at the local dive bar and drank beer until they couldn't stomach any more. She and Jonathan had a whirlwind romantic relationship and she wanted to continue that into their marriage.

Although Kelly didn't have a great example of family growing up, she knew what she hoped for and that's exactly what she had.

After they finished dinner Jonathan prepared the girls for bed while Kelly ran comps for a few homes that she wanted to share with a prospective client in the morning.

It didn't take long for them to get themselves together and leave their apartment. By the time the sitter reached their door, they were wearing their jackets and ready to leave.

The cab ride to the restaurant was quiet as they relaxed in each other's arms watching the city wake up. Sure it was dark outside, but she was well aware that unlike her daughters who were home snoring in their beds, the city was just stirring awake. It was after 9pm in Manhattan.

"I want to become a Preacher," Jonathan said as Kelly stared at him open mouthed. She hadn't had an opportunity to place the first sweet and tangy, soft and creamy morsel on her tongue before he hit her with the big news.

"What?" she asked as he continued talking excited and oblivious to her befuddled look.

"Remember I told you about the Sunday service at my grandfather's church? Kelly, it was so powerful. I just can't stop thinking about it and ever since then...I don't know I feel at peace," he said, reaching across the table to take her hand in his. "I know this is sudden and I wouldn't ordinarily drop something on you like this, but I feel so passionate about this, honey," he said looking deeply into her eyes.

She watched as he passionately detailed how he realized that he was called to share his testimony with the world. "I don't know how I'll do this. I don't know where to begin. I just know that I have to," he said. Jonathan began to explain the story of Jonah to his wife. Jonah suffered because he kept running away from what God had planned for him. He wanted her to understand that this was his divine purpose.

"Well, I support anything that you believe in Jonathan. We are a team. You and me and no one else. I would be wrong if I told you not to follow your destiny. Just tell me what you need me to do," she said as he smiled at her sweetly.

She truly was his angel. Jonathan couldn't have wished for a better wife. Kelly was his Superwoman. No matter what she was going through, she always supported and encouraged him. He teased Kelly that she saved him from a life of loneliness and misery.

It was true.

Kelly's upbeat spirit and motivating attitude were like sunshine on a rainy day. Her words simply warmed him on the inside, causing him to believe in himself.

Gazing into her lively blue eyes, Jonathan wished that he could marry his wife all over again. He took her hand gently in his and planted a soft kiss on it. "You have no idea how much you mean to me," he said as she giggled.

"I just need you to be you," he said with a bright smile. He took a hunk of cheesecake and popped it in his mouth with a satisfying smile, "Just keep being you," he repeated.

2 Thessalonians 3:13

"But ye, brethren, be not weary in well doing."

Chapter 26

Angela couldn't remember a day when she was more nervous. She never considered herself an extrovert. In grade school, she wasn't the social butterfly. Angela found herself in the corner with a good book most of the time. She chuckled nervously as she recalled her first day of high school, many years ago.

She was a complete ball of nerves. Her mother had to give her anxiety medication to leave the house. Today felt just as nerve wracking as the day she stepped on the high school campus and looked around at the crowd of students.

This time she refused to turn around and run back home. Angela was determined to make it through her first day, jitters and all. She would make herself and her son proud by doing something completely different.

She wasn't afraid of any challenge, she just had to get through the first day and everything else would be smooth sailing. At least that's what she told herself.

The rain pounded on her roof providing a melodic background to Angela's panic episode. She couldn't get herself together. Her heart was pounding and her palms were sweating like she had to perform a symphony in front of thousands, she was a complete wreck.

Angela paced in front of the mirror, smoothing her blouse over her long skirt. She was preparing for her first day of class and she couldn't wait, but she was also very nervous. Angela hadn't attended school in over three decades. She was a grandmother, what made her think that she could do this?

She decided to take off her clothes and toss on her comfy PJs. The rain outside was a perfect excuse to relax in bed with the Golden Girls on Netflix. Instead, she glanced at the scripture hanging on her wall, Philippians 4:13 – "I can do ALL things through Christ who strengthens me".

Angela let out a loud sigh when her doorbell suddenly rang. Walking to the front door, wondering who would be visiting her unannounced she opened the door and was pleasantly surprised to see Anna.

"So, I figured you might need some first day of school motivation," she said raising a cup of coffee in the air. "Guess what, I registered for a pottery class at the same time as your course. We are directly across the hall from each other," she announced as the two women squealed with delight.

Anna was tired of sitting in the house and sulking about not finding a husband in her late 30s and being lonely. After Angela told her that she registered for a class at the community center, she decided to look into their Fall Catalog.

She was so glad that she did.

"Thank you for coming by Anna. I really needed the support," she said grabbing the Starbucks coffee from her hand and taking a gratifying sip. "Hmm...thank you," she said.

"Are you ready to go," Anna asked eagerly.

Angela grabbed her oversized bag and slung it over her shoulder. She had a bag packed with art supplies, her journal and iPad. Angela was prepared to have an amazing day. When they walked outside the clouds were parting and the sun began to shine. Smiling at the sky both women simultaneously spoke, "Thank you," they said to the sky.

They were about to embark on something new in their lives and they couldn't have thought of anyone else to share the new experience with. Angela was still in physical therapy for her injury, but luckily she didn't injure her dominate arm. She was growing stronger everyday and she was grateful for it.

Her doctor was impressed and so was Anna. Angela's fall and recovery was nothing short of a testimony to God's healing power.

Psalm 46:10

"Be still, and know that I am God: I will be exalted among the heathen, I will be exalted in the earth."

Chapter 27

The cold sterile room make Kelly shudder. She wrapped her arms around herself and took in a deep breath. Kelly was convinced that she was carrying a boy this time. She couldn't wait to give her husband the amazing news. Kelly figured that their family was due for some exciting and wonderful news.

She imagined how her daughters would react to the news of a new baby. Brianna would be beside herself. Brittany would want to help with everything. They would be great big sisters. Kelly couldn't wait for it all. She thought about the colors they would paint the nursery, then shoved the idea aside.

The world was moving towards "gender neutral" things. She wondered how Jonathan would feel about an all neutral baby nursery. It would be an interesting change from the basic blue or pink nursery, but Kelly wasn't sold on the idea.

Every year the mainstream world came up with new and innovative ways to make raising children more chic. Kelly knew that Jonathan wouldn't be interested in fads. He would insist that their son's room be painted blue. She laughed at the thought of their nursery painting conversation, "everything will be perfect," she said.

Suddenly, a feeling of fear washed over Kelly. Kelly felt terrified. Her heart beat quickened and she began to sweat profusely. "What if everything is not alright?" she said to herself. She imagined the worse and tried her hardest to push the negative ideas out of her head before the doctor came in.

"Dear God, I pray that everything is alright," she said aloud as she waited patiently for her doctor to enter the room. When Dr. Cumberbach finally entered the room, she appeared somber.

"You're not pregnant," the doctor said with a sadness in her voice. She knew how eager her patient sounded about being a mother for the third time. Kelly all but said it during her last visit. Placing an encouraging hand on Kelly's shoulder Dr. Cumberbach shook her head sadly, "I'm sorry," she said as Kelly drew in a breath, preparing for the rest of her test results.

"Kelly, your platelet count are extremely low. We would like to run a few additional tests on you. I'm going to order a bone marrow aspiration and review," she said as gently as she possibly could. Kelly tried to hold her composure but the mere mention of bone marrow scans and aspirations sent her on a completely different planet.

She wished that she would've brought Jonathan along with her. He would have known exactly what to do and say to keep her comforted. Instead she was crying a river on her doctor's shoulder. "Kelly, there is no cause for panic. We are just doing some tests to be sure," she reassured as Kelly nodded in agreement.

"My staff will schedule you an appointment with the hospital to have the bone marrow exam completed. We are just doing a test to rule out everything, Kelly. Your blood work concerned us and we just want to dive a bit deeper," she said rubbing Kelly's shoulder. "I like to be cautious," she assured.

After her doctor left Kelly sat on the edge of the cold examination table with her face in her hands. She was devastated. Not only was she not pregnant now she had to worry about an intrusive exam. She took the referrals and paperwork from the receptionist and walked out of the office trying not to look at the paper.

Hebrews 4:16

"Let us therefore come boldly unto the throne of grace, that we may obtain mercy, and find grace to help in time of need."

Chapter 28

"I have to get a bone marrow scan," she blurted out the minute he wrapped his arms around her tiny body. He didn't respond, he just held her tighter. Jonathan didn't know that she had a doctors appointment and he felt terrible for not being there with her. Feeling his strength sustaining her body, she finally let go. It was all she could do after the day she'd experienced.

The floodgates opened and tears poured out as she sobbed. She told him everything; about her thoughts of being pregnant again and about her follow-up appointment. Although the pain from the conversation was overwhelming so was the relief from unloading all of the trauma she felt.

"I'm scared," she whispered as he agreed with her. "Me too," he admitted. Jonathan didn't want to consider what would happen to his family if his wife was ill. She was the backbone of their family. No one did anything without Kelly scheduling, researching and arranging. Their family thrived because of the way they complimented each other.

Jonathan had to reassure his wife that everything would be fine. He also had to reassure himself. "God is a healer. He is faithful, Kelly. We just need to pray," he comforted as she cried. "Pray," she asked leaning back from his embrace to look him in the eyes.

He was more comfortable with prayer and religion that she was. Her parents didn't expose her to any aspect of religion and her father was a staunch atheist so she never cared to learn anything about faith and God. She panicked when Jonathan stated that they needed to pray. Kelly was afraid of looking awkward. What if she said the wrong thing?

She didn't know how to pray.

She tried to do it, but felt silly. Together, that night they both held hands and closed their eyes as they rested on their knees praying to God. Kelly felt uneasy but she listened to the words that her husband spoke. The way he talked to God as if he were his father sitting right beside him.

It all seemed surreal to her.

She wondered what it would take for her to have a relationship with God where she could just simply talk to him and trust that he heard her. For the first time in Kelly's life she felt security wrapped tight around her as she slept.

She acknowledged it as the peace of God. She also acknowledged one other fact, her husband would make an amazing preacher. It was in that moment where her frantic, frightened heart gave way to peace that she realized her husband's faith would help sustain them. It was at that moment when Kelly realized that her husband was the best thing that could have ever happened to her. Jonathan and his relationship with God calmed her spirit and her mind.

Their faith in God would keep them protected, she was sure of it.

John 15:11

"These things have I spoken unto you, that my joy might remain in you, and that your joy might be full."

Chapter 29

"So how was your first day," Anna asked as they munched on French fries at the mall food court. Angela took a bite of the pizza slice and beamed with pride. "It was awesome," she said reliving her first time back in school since the 70s. "I love the class. I am already learning new techniques," she said pulling out her pad to show Anna what she'd learned so far.

Anna was impressed by Angela's talent and her enthusiasm.

"There are only eight of us in the class so we really get attention from the professor without having to worry about being seen," she said happily. "And he's adorable. He reminds me of Jonathan," she said with a smile. "He's a young fellow but very patient and understanding," she said as Anna listened intently.

The sound of Jonathan's name took Anna back to a different time. She cared for him deeply but would never confess her feelings about him to anyone. He was happily married after all and she was still waiting on God to send her Boaz. She knew that it was only a matter of time. All she had to do was work on herself and her walk with God. Anna's focus remained on the Living Waters Baptist Church and dedicating herself to the work that was placed on her heart. Everything else would fall into place. God never broke his promises.

She listened with glee as Angela spoke. Seeing her mentor in higher spirits lifted her mood. Anna enjoyed her class, but it was mainly to keep her entertained and out of the house. Truthfully, she scheduled the class to keep an eye on Angela. She was still worried about her after finding her right after her fall. Anna was devastated by the thought of losing Angela. It was Angela who helped Anna out of a dark place when her friends were getting married and having children; she helped her see that her job in the kingdom was more important than her biological clock.

Anna vowed that she would keep a closer eye on Angela from that point forward. Angela was the closest person she had to a real mother daughter relationship. Although her mother was in her life, they didn't have a real relationship. Her mother was a malignant narcissist amongst other things so she didn't know how to nurture her daughter. They kept their distance from each other on purpose.

Every conversation ended in an explosion no matter the reason. Her mother didn't understand her and she didn't make an effort to try. Instead she reminded her daughter that being married to the church would be her imminent doom.

Anna's parents split right after she graduated from high school. Her father disappeared to Florida and aside from the occasional post card from Daytona Beach she didn't hear from him often. Her mother was a completely different story.

Driven to depression after the divorce, Anna's mother never recovered mentally. She went into full break down mode and spent the fifteen years in a psychiatric facility. She couldn't have visitors and spent most of her time alternating between manic and depressive episodes of bipolar rage. It was the most heartbreaking thing ever.

Her mother's favorite target was Anna. She found herself defending every decision she made after high school. In her mother's opinion she wasted her entire life and would not be stuck living as a nun forever.

Anna visited her mother twice. Once when she was committed to the facility and her final time when her mother accused her of shattering their marriage. Her mother took a swing at Anna and had to be physically restrained. Anna had enough with her mother after that devastating moment. Anna didn't care how sick her mother was, she was done with her after that.

Anna avoided contact with her mother for her own self preservation, although it broke her heart to know that she would never have a loving relationship with her parents. It hurt Anna to come to that realization after years of trying to ignore the cold, hard facts. She spent every holiday alone until Angela opened her arms, her home and her heart.

She was essentially an orphan.

That's why she held on tight to Angela. She was her lifeline.

2 Corinthians 4:16-18

"For which cause we faint not; but though our outward man perish, yet the inward man is renewed day by day. [17] For our light affliction, which is but for a moment, worketh for us a far more exceeding and eternal weight of glory; [18] While we look not at the things which are seen, but at the things which are not seen: for the things which are seen are temporal; but the things which are not seen are eternal."

Chapter 30

Kelly wrapped herself with the warm blankets supplied by the friendly brunette nurse with the earnest smile. She made sure that Kelly was comfortable as they prepared for her procedure. After being poked, prodded and MRI'd to death, Kelly was heading into her last exam.

She prayed that after this test her doctor would know what was plaguing her health. Her tests already proved that she was severely anemic and deficient in many nutrients. That explained her exhaustion. She was up all night researching the medical possibilities. Jonathan had to beg her to log off the computer and simply trust God for the outcome.

She was a nervous wreck.

As the medication began to ease through her veins she rested her head on the hard pillow and began to drift off to sleep. "I love you, Kelly. You will be fine, just trust God," Jonathan whispered in her ear as he squeezed her hand.

The doctors wheeled his wife out of the room as he said a silent prayer for her. Reaching in his pocket he pulled out his phone to call his grandfather. Just as he scrolled through his contacts, his phone vibrated in his hand. Luke's picture came across the screen causing Jonathan to laugh. "Right on time," he said chuckling as his grandfather laughed heartily.

"I was just thinking about you and you called me," he said. "What's going on son," his grandfather asked after they chatted about everything from the weather to the their college football picks.

"Where are you," his grandfather asked as he heard the voices on the overhead speaker in the background of Jonathan's phone. "I'm in the hospital, Pop. Kelly is having tests done and well, I'm worried," he confessed as his grandfather began to pray.

"Be there for her when she comes out of the procedure. Encourage her like you've encouraged our congregation," he advised as Jonathan listened intently. "Pray over your wife. You two pray together every night," he added.

They talked for a while longer before Luke exclaimed, "That's what I forgot. Guess what," he asked playfully. "The Greater Mount Zion Church in Duluth has requested *our* presence at their revival service next month. I just received the invitation. It appears that your testimony has grown legs, son," he said congratulating his grandson.

"Really," Jonathan exclaimed with delight. He was beyond thrilled. He and his wife recently decided to make a life changing, career altering decision and now he was being invited to speak at a church. It was divine intervention to Jonathan. Just when he was about to give up, God tossed him a lifeline.

He had his confirmation.

"Pastor Saxby called me personally to invite us," he said beaming with pride. "Take your time and pray over your decision. I know that you and Kelly have a lot going on right now. I just wanted you to know that. I love you," he said ending the conversation so Jonathan could go back to the waiting area in the hospital.

He sat in the seat proud as ever.

Psalm 5:11

"But let all those that put their trust in thee rejoice: let them ever shout for joy, because thou defendest them: let them also that love thy name be joyful in thee."

Chapter 31

Anna rested in her car and changed the radio station. She listened to smooth jazz as she drove home replaying Angela's words. The mere mention of Jonathan's name sent her heart fluttering. She tried to mask it from Angela. She couldn't risk being found out as someone who was in love with a man who was unavailable to her.

Sure she dated men and had a few boyfriends but no one held her heart like Jonathan. He was the only person to actually understand the real, Anna; not the person that she presented to the world. Jonathan took the time to know Anna and care about her. She will forever be grateful to him for showing her how real love felt.

Anna couldn't have imagined what her life would have been without the Flannigan family. They loved her because they loved Jonathan. The Flannigan's collectively helped bring her closer to God which ultimately saved her life. Especially Jonathan. Even in the midst of his struggles with acceptance, finding himself and becoming who God wanted him to be, he still found the time to minister to her.

When he refused to follow her down the path of destruction, she began to wise up. When they were together last, she tried to get him to steal for her. Although he was willing to push the envelope a bit, he outright abhorred things that called his personal integrity into jeopardy. He wouldn't harm another human, intentionally. That wasn't how Jonathan was raised and he refused to be a part of it with Anna.

When he refused she teased him in jest.

It didn't go over well. Jonathan lost respect for his friend that day. When he saw that she was willing to do anything even harm innocent people just for a thrill, it disappointed him. Anna wasn't poor or destitute, she just lacked a strong moral compass.

His feelings for her changed that day and she could clearly see it in his eyes. That realization shook her to the core.

The look of disgust on his face, changed her life forever. It changed the way that she looked at herself. Anna watched as Jonathan straightened himself out and graduated high school without a glance in her direction.

She felt ashamed for behaving like she didn't care about anything. Anna decided to take charge of her life and change the trajectory of it. She dedicated her life to Christ and He truly kept her in the palm of his hand.

Her parents were devout Christians but by her graduation both had stopped attending regular services, opting to listen to the radio at home on Sundays. It didn't take long for her nuclear family to crumble after they removed their Christian faith from their marriage.

Anna had to witness the demise of her parents relationship, first hand. She rejoiced when the divorce was finalized. No one else understood how she felt, but she decided to stay in Minnesota after her mother's mental health began to deteriorate she moved her in to a two bedroom apartment. They sold the family home and her father moved to Florida.

Just like that, in a matter of several days her entire childhood was dismantled in front of her eyes. It was devastating and she felt so alone, but that was when she leaned on Jesus.

She cared for her mother as best as she could, but realized that her mother was a danger to herself and others. She made the traumatizing decision to have her mother admitted to the local psychiatric hospital for 72 hours.

Anna realized that God took her to a point of nearly losing her mind in order to change her mind. She lost everything, her support, her parents and the love of her life. She lost it all but found God and he's been holding her hand ever since.

Her willingness to grow as a Christian and her grief from Jonathan's move to New York made her and Angela fast friends. They were both going through their own battles of loneliness when they decided to team up for the church bowling league. Angela went from a friend's mother, to a mentor to someone she fondly referred to as, Mom.

For that Anna was grateful.

Joshua 1:8

"This book of the law shall not depart out of thy mouth; but thou shalt meditate therein day and night, that thou mayest observe to do according to all that is written therein: for then thou shalt make thy way prosperous, and then thou shalt have good success."

Chapter 32

Jonathan prayed for his family as they stood together in a circle. Brianna held his hand and she closed her eyes tightly. Her sister said, "Amen" at the conclusion of their prayer, loud and proudly. This was how the Flannigan household prepared to leave their home each day.

Things had changed in their home. He and Kelly worked with the girls at night to teach them how to pray. It was adorable and comical at the same time. The girls didn't have an understanding of whom they were praying too, but Jonathan felt like every little bit helped.

They read the Children's Bible together and channeled his father's spirit to retell fantastic stories from the Bible with animation. His girls were just as engrossed in his story as he was when he was a child listening to his father talk about the three men thrown in the furnace or the story about Moses and the Ten Commandments.

Each night the story changed, but the lesson remained the same, God was a protector, a healer, a deliverer and our all.

Kelly listened to his teachings and followed along. It felt wonderful to learn about God and His love for them. The more she learned the hungrier she grew for knowledge. Since their family didn't own a Bible, they took a trip to the local Christian Book store to select one.

The New Life Application Bible had an easy to follow study guide that she used extensively. She took notes and studied just like she was told to in Joshua 1:8 – "Study to show thyself approved..." became her favorite biblical scripture.

When she dined alone at lunch she pulled out her Bible and studied. She used Bible Journaling techniques to make her studies more exciting, using highlighters, pens and post-it notes. Studying the Bible was more important to her than studying her exam materials for the Realtor exam.

Kelly was captivated.

She began reading the Bible enthusiastically. The more she read the more encouraged she grew about Jonathan's walk in life. The story of John the Baptist touched her heart. Although, he had many challenges against him he still carried out the will of God by leading his people out of captivity into their promised land.

After considering Moses and how he brought so many souls out of bondage, she couldn't keep silent about Jonathan's planned endeavors. She wanted Jonathan to visit churches and tell his story.

One night as they studied the Bible together she glanced at her husband and said, "I think you should go," she said as he stopped reading and looked at her. "Your grandfather wants you to attend the revival service at the church and I think you should go. You never know what God has in store for you," she advised.

Jonathan listened to his wife's wisdom. He hadn't considered his grandfather's offer since their phone conversation. Jonathan didn't want to leave his wife and daughters in New York to fly across the country again, but he knew that he had an assignment.

At that moment, Kelly confirmed it.

"I will keep things together in New York," she added referring to the girls and their home. He didn't need reassurance of that from her. Kelly was always the home manager and kept everyone moving to their assigned tasks.

Her pursuit of Biblical knowledge had encompassed the entire family.

She found research tools and crossword puzzles to help her understand the Bible better and she was on a roll. Jonathan was pleased to see his wife willing to learn something new. He wondered if he would've been so pliable if he wasn't raised a Christian.

The stories that he told his daughters, the books of the Bible that they studied together jogged his memory to a time when he and his parents would study the Bible together. His father collected artifacts from across the globe so that enhanced his studies even more. Instead of hearing about the clay pots that were used during those times, he actually got to touch one and see it with his own eyes.

He saw pictures of the places that his father actually visited in Jerusalem and Egypt, places that some would only see in their imaginations, his father brought it all home to his son and his wife. It was awe inspiring watching how his parents communicated and related over Biblical scripture. His grandfather would join in and they would debate their theories on the Bible. It was a fascinating time.

Jonathan learned more from watching his parents and grandfather interact with each other than he learned sitting in the front pew of the Living Waters Baptist Church. He didn't know it then, but it was all preparation for his promotion.

2 Corinthians 5:20

"Now then we are ambassadors for Christ, as though God did beseech you by us: we pray you in Christ's stead, be ye reconciled to God."

Chapter 33

"I witnessed what the world would be like without a God and it was the scariest most traumatic event of my life. It changed me forever," Jonathan said as he began his testimony. Even though he'd shared his testimony hundreds of times before, every time he did it felt like the first time.

"There was widespread famine and wars in places that once held peace. The Earth was consumed with fire. I witnessed the public going wild and crazy. They relished in the fact that there was no God. No one to oversee their sin and filth. It was a horrible sight," Jonathan said as he began to talk about the sins he witnessed. He noticed the reaction of the congregation.

He saw the look of fear wash across their faces, as people heard about a life without God, a life where their faith was deemed irrelevant. It seemed unfathomable to them. When he spoke of his time in Jerusalem and how God brought him out of the pit, a believer, they applauded with joy.

He talked about his father and how he wanted to become an archeologist like the infamous, Brad Flannigan, but God had different plans. Even when he went in the opposite direction of God's plan by choosing to go to Jerusalem to scientifically disprove Christianity, God still preserved his life.

He noticed how the crowd celebrated his testimony. Everyone loved a comeback story; a story of redemption. Everyone loved to hear about Jonathan's testimony, but no one wanted to hear about the revelations that he saw. When he discussed how the world looked without a God, he noticed how the congregation shifted in their seats.

Their looks of fear turned to looks of disbelief. He watched as some people stood and left the sanctuary while he spoke. No one wanted to hear about anything this heavy, he could see it on their faces. They came to have their ears tickled about prosperity and redemption. No one anticipated that Jonathan would talk about sin.

Who wants to talk about sin?

At the close of his testimony, Jonathan left the podium to a less than stellar response. There was no standing ovation or thunderous applause. In fact, he heard a few folks booing in the back of the building.

When he stepped off the stage, the Church Administrator promptly asked to speak with him in private. Byron Stanley was the tall, balding man wearing a black Armani suit and a look of supreme displeasure. Byron complained to Jonathan and berated him for trying to sermonize his testimony. "I assure you that if we had known what you were speaking on we wouldn't have invited you," he said with a frown.

Jonathan didn't know what to say. He stood there for a while in shock then he responded, "I came here to tell the congregation about God. I have a mission to warn everyone about the visions I saw," he said as the man chuckled.

"Visions?" he said raising his perfectly arched eyebrow. "You sir are a lunatic. I wish you could have heard yourself ranting and raving on the stage like some madman. We don't scare our congregation into believing here at Clearview Baptist," he said with a huff.

Jonathan left the church feeling devastated.

When he first told his testimony he was standing in his grandfather's church, Living Waters Baptist Church it was a humbling experience for him. Suddenly after that first testimony he found himself traveling around the country sharing and ministering to others.

Jonathan didn't expect the same reception that he received at Living Waters Baptist Church. It was his home church, his grandfather's church of course they received him well. He definitely didn't anticipate some of the negativity he received by surrounding area churches. Some churches didn't want him to talk to their parishioners. They declined his invitations.

He pressed onward with his mission, but he decided to change it up a bit.

It all started at Greater Mount Zion. The Greater Mount Zion Church in Duluth, Minnesota was hosting Living Waters Baptist Church at their revival service and Jonathan was moving the congregation with his story.

Once it was all over, he found himself overtaken with parishioners and visitors who wanted to share their experiences with him. His grandfather stood next to him watching in awe. He was amazed at how Jonathan's story brought out so much in others. His story was so real and raw. He wasn't ashamed to tell others that the grandson of a preacher, one of the most infamous Preachers in Minnesota was an Atheist for years.

His truth was astounding. It evoked an emotion from people that Luke rarely saw. He wasn't the only person who took notice of Jonathan's testimony. Reverend Dr. Clyde Moore from the New Life International Christian Conference also heard Jonathan speak and he was riveted.

People were praying and thanking God for saving Jonathan. His story of redemption was encouraging for everyone who heard it. The altar was filled with people rededicating their life to Christ.

It was beautiful.

After the service, he caught up with Jonathan and introduced himself. He gave Jonathan his card and told him to call him to set up a meeting. He wanted to offer Jonathan the chance of a lifetime.

Two months had gone by and Jonathan had seen and slept in every hotel in the nation. He could start his own travel review website with the amount of hotels he frequented and airlines he'd traveled on.

Everything was beginning to settle in his life. He traveled on the weekends and worked long days and nights at his position in the law firm to make it all work, but it worked. He was proud to be able to hold everything together.

His mother was healing well and his daughters were blossoming. He and Kelly were planning to travel for their wedding anniversary which was coming up in a few days. They decided at the last minute to take the girls with them instead of hiring a sitter.

Jonathan had an appearance in Texas and decided to fly the entire family there for the weekend.

It all seemed so perfect, but Jonathan knew that it wasn't. Jonathan was still haunted at night with nightmares, because he knew that he wasn't doing what God expected. He was still sugarcoating the message.

2 Timothy 2:15

"Study to shew thyself approved unto God, a workman that needeth not to be ashamed, rightly dividing the word of truth."

Chapter 34

The Texas sun shined brightly as they all exited the plane onto the tarmac. The 90 degree weather was a drastic contrast to the 60 degree temperatures that they just left in New York. Jonathan looked towards the sun with a smile, loving the warmth.

Brianna was mesmerized by the entire travel experience. Being only five, she wasn't used to traveling on airplanes. Brittany was tired from the flight so she slept as Jonathan carried her through the airport to their awaiting Uber.

Kelly was feeling tired but she didn't want to disappoint Jonathan. Every weekend he had a different speaking engagement so he was rarely home from Friday to Monday and when he was home he tried to cram as much family time in as possible.

She cherished those times. He talked endlessly about his experiences, the people he met and the stories he heard. Every time he returned home he seemed even more grateful to be there with her and the girls.

She could tell that he saw it in her eyes, so she tried to add more pep to her voice when she spoke. With Jonathan traveling she didn't want to concern him and make him stay at home fussing over her.

His job was too great.

She just doubled up on her vitamins, hoping that would help. As they met the driver at the airport exit she nearly leaped for joy. Kelly couldn't wait to sit down and take a quick nap, she hoped that her husband didn't have too much planned for them.

When the cab pulled up to the hotel entrance Jonathan helped Kelly out of the car and then he unbuckled his daughter's from their seats. They were bubbling with excitement and eager to hop out of the car and see Texas. He watched them drag their Hello Kitty suitcases behind them as they walked laughing.

They checked in to the hotel room and settled their belongings in their rooms. After checking on the girls he opened the door to the adjoining hotel room to check on Kelly.

Jonathan missed his family.

Being on the road was a great experience, but there was nothing more fulfilling than coming home to a loving family. He pulled his suitcase to the side of the room and turned around searching for Kelly.

When he walked in the bathroom he found her, lying on the floor in a crumbled heap. Jonathan quickly sprang into action running to his wife's aid. She was barely conscious. "Kelly," he screamed in fear. Something serious was wrong with his wife.

His heart leapt when he saw her open her eyes.

"Are you alright," he asked as she tried to lift her head to respond then suddenly she passed out again in his arms.

Psalm 34:18

"The Lord is nigh unto them that are of a broken heart; and saveth such as be of a contrite spirit."

Chapter 35

Holding hands in the cold waiting room, Kelly shivered and wrapped the shawl around her shoulders snuggly. Although, they didn't know what to expect at the appointment, they both had faith. They prayed about the outcome on their way to the doctor's appointment. After they dropped the girls off at daycare she and Jonathan went to breakfast before her appointment.

At breakfast, Jonathan bubbled over with excitement talking about the many different people he met during his travels to Minnesota. He was ready to head back out there and tell everyone about his testimony and how God saved him. His excitement was contagious. They forgot about Kelly's doctor appointment as they plotted and planned how Jonathan could manage being an Evangelist and an attorney.

He didn't want to consider quitting his job. It was their foundation. He questioned if they could make it in a city like New York without his job.

"Well let's move to Minnesota," Kelly pondered as Jonathan considered her words.

They shared a nervous laugh and both said, "Nah" at the same time shaking their heads. After living in a city like New York he wasn't sure if he could uproot his family and move to the slower Midwest. He enjoyed the hustle and bustle of the city, the multicultural experience.

His daughters had friends in their classes who spoke, Swahili and Mandarin. They learned about different people just by interacting with them on a daily basis, not by the biases of the news or media. It was enriching and fulfilling to Jonathan, a child who was raised in the Midwest.

Jonathan and Kelly loved that idea. That was one of the reasons why they chose to live in an expensive luxury apartment in New York instead of a modest home in the country.

"Flannigan" the nurse called out as Kelly and Jonathan both stood at attention. They were anxious to hear her doctor's findings. As they walked down the red carpeted hallway towards the doctor's office he squeezed her hand gently to let her know that he was right there with her.

The slim doctor made her way into the room greeting them both with a warm handshake. Then she noticed two additional people standing behind her. She remembered the tall skinny guy with the short curly hair cut from the hospital. His office performed several blood screening tests on her.

He was Dr. Consuela, her hematologist. She only visited him twice but she found him to be extremely gentle. She wondered, *Why was he here? Who was the other doctor?*

Everything seemed to happen so fast, but everyone was talking in slow motion.

After the first MRI scan she began to block the tests and faces out of her mind. It was reminiscent of her battle with breast cancer several years prior. She tried not to consider the possibility that the cancer may have returned. Drawing in a breath she stilled herself, trying not to cry because she knew that it would upset her husband.

Dr. Cumberbach opened Kelly's folder, glanced at the information and sat down behind her desk. "Kelly, I brought you in here to tell you about your test results. We conducted a full screening to rule out serious illness," she said as she chose her words meticulously.

 "We would like to schedule you for surgery immediately to assess the situation," she began as Kelly jumped. "Surgery, for what?" she shrieked in fear. "Your platelets are dangerously low, your red blood cell count is off and the bone marrow aspiration showed a few things that concerned us," her doctor said carefully eyeing Jonathan and Kelly's reaction.

"This is Dr. Keaton. He is an oncology surgeon and he will be joining our care team," she said as the short portly older gentleman leaned forward and offered her a sweaty hand to shake. He looked her in the eyes and she could feel his concern for her. There was something soothing about him that made her feel comfortable.

She recited the Lord's Prayer quietly in her mind as the doctors continued talking about tumors, surgery and tests. It was happening all over again, déjà vu. This time she had a weapon, she had prayer on her side.

When she fought breast cancer the last time she felt hopeless. She didn't know God. She didn't know that there was power and healing in his name. Now that she was confident in his healing power, she tried to meditate and focus on Him.

Even in the middle of her own living nightmare.

"We hope to remove the tumor and start you on an aggressive form of radiation for several weeks," her doctor continued speaking robotically. She knew that the news was devastating but she had to inform her patient.

Kelly began to hyperventilate as her husband rubbed her back. Dr. Cumberbach offered her a tissue from the small box on her desk. This was the worst part of her job. She hated having to tell people things like this. The team of specialists was her idea. She figured that they could help ease her anxieties by explaining to her their initial plan for testing.

She cleared her throat as Kelly pressed the doctors for a prognosis. She couldn't speak, her mouth was dry, but her eyes were watering. This was not the first time she felt such strong emotions for a patient. She liked the Flannigan family, and it made her sad to think that she would have to witness Kelly endure treatment again.

Psalm 119:114

"Thou art my hiding place and my shield: I hope in thy word."

Chapter 36

"Cancer," she said aloud as her husband said a silent prayer. "Cancer," she repeated staring off into space. Kelly broke down sobbing as she considered the sad reality. "Jonathan, I don't know if I can go through this again," she said shaking her head. "We have two beautiful daughters that I may not see grow up," she said as they walked hand in hand in Central Park.

"Who will be there to watch them get dressed for their prom? I don't want to miss my daughter's wedding or their first baby!" she cried as Jonathan tried to console his wife. He had to calm his own raging fears to help comfort his wife.

Jonathan couldn't hear Kelly talk about her own death. It scared him to death. Jonathan needed her to be the optimistic voice that he counted on. If Kelly lost all hope and fell into despair, what would happen to his family?

They depended on Kelly for everything. Jonathan slyly wiped away a tear before he cleared his throat and steadied his voice. He didn't want her to hear his voice and his resolve cracking.

"Don't think about that right now, Kelly. Let's see what happens after the surgery and their treatment plan is concluded. We don't know enough to panic yet," he assured as she continued mulling over the words of her doctor. Jonathan was grateful that his wife couldn't see his tears as he embraced her.

"But regardless, I'm right here. I won't move from your side," he assured her as he held her in his arms. "Promise me that you won't stop doing God's work," she pleaded as he lowered his head in sadness. "I promise to never leave your side," he said as he kissed her lovingly.

"This is your destiny," she said wiping away a tear.

He understood what she meant but he couldn't agree to that promise. The minute he heard the word, Cancer his life changed. He decided at that moment not to hop on another plane unless his wife had a clean bill of health.

A tumor in her breast?

They had to do something to take their minds off of Kelly's appointment so they decided to take an afternoon walk in the park but they couldn't help worrying about it. Both of them were shocked by the diagnosis.

Jonathan felt hopeful, since the doctors seemed very positive about her prognosis.

He also knew how doctors and surgeons spoke. Everything was absolute and certain, there was little room for guessing in their profession. So he knew for sure that they were certain about the tumors. His mind drifted back to Kelly's first breast cancer treatment.

The entire ordeal almost cost them their home, their sanity and most importantly his wife's life. It wasn't something that he wanted to consider as a possibility. He recalled how they rejoiced when the cancer went into remission. He planned to do the same thing only bigger this time, he would take his wife on a trip around the world.

They just had to make it through the next several months of treatment.

Romans 12:12

"Rejoicing in hope; patient in tribulation; continuing instant in prayer."

Chapter 37

Anna and Angela sat in front of the television guessing the prices of the items on the screen in front of them. They had just returned from the community center where they were both enjoying their classes, respectively.

Angela loved painting so much that she had an easel in the corner of her living room, beside the Steinway. She loved making music and enjoyed playing on the piano often, but there was something soothing about painting that she craved.

She was delighted to meet new friends in the class. She met Charles on the first day of class. When she first entered the room she had to stave off a panic attack by breathing deeply. It felt like the first day of third grade all over again. She didn't know anyone in the room and desperately wanted to bolt out of there, but instead she took a deep breath, settled her resolve and walked to an empty seat and sat down.

Charles walked in the class two minutes after her and she could tell by the look on his face that he was experiencing his own personal first day of school nightmare.

When he sat down he smiled at her warmly and reached inside of his knapsack for a pencil and pad. She eyed him as he pulled out his phone to and began tapping at the screen. Suddenly the phone began to vibrate in his hands causing him to nearly drop it.

After fumbling with the phone for several seconds, he grabbed it and answered quickly, "hello," he whispered. "Yes, I made it. I'm fine," the several seconds later he repeated himself. "I'm fine. I'll see you after class," he said hanging up the phone.

He noticed Angela looking his way and smiled, "my granddaughter treats me like I'm her child," he said shrugging his shoulders as they laughed together. "Ah, the circle of life I guess," he surmised as they both shared a chuckle.

She liked her classmates. They were all mature aged so they didn't have to worry about being left behind by the computer generation. They were able to take the course at their own pace, except for the initial introductory course that required online access.

Angela thought she would die of embarrassment, but like always God sent someone to her rescue. Charles made her feel at ease when she didn't understand how to log in to the computerized system to begin the introductory course.

There was also her new friend, Edna an energetic woman with bright red hair and freckles. She had an honest look about her and a genuine smile that drew anyone in.

Edna was a recently widowed when her husband of thirty years died from Alzheimer related complications. She was determined to keep her wits about her so she decided to take on a few classes to get herself out of the house. Edna and Angela became fast friends.

Their most recent outing was to the movie theater, a place that neither of the ladies had visited in years. It was a welcomed treat to be able to kick back with popcorn and enjoy a show.

Edna suggested that they do something more exciting and Angela was all ears. They found themselves at the Go-Kart track driving around the track as fast as they could, squealing with delight.

Job 13:15

"Though he slay me, yet will I trust in him: but I will maintain mine own ways before him."

Chapter 38

Jonathan paced the floor as he prayed silently for strength. His wife had been in surgery for three hours and the doctors still were operating on her. There was no word about how long they would be. He considered calling his grandfather for counsel but figured it would be best to talk to him once they knew everything.

They agreed not to let anyone know about Kelly's health until they had all of the information to answer the questions that he was sure would be tossed at them from everyone who cared about them.

That decision left him feeling alone when he really could have used his mother's calming voice to ground his emotions. Instead, he opened the Bible and began to read over his notes from the study session he had with Kelly the night prior. Even though he could tell that she was worried about the surgery, watching her faith and determination to learn about the word of God was inspiring.

He was so engrossed in his notes that he didn't see the surgeon standing in front of him until the portly man cleared his throat. Jonathan jumped up to greet the doctor and to barrage him with his questions. "How did everything go? Is she alright," he asked as his questions flowed together causing one large rambling sentence of confusion. The surgeon smiled calmly. "Your wife is in recovery. We were able to remove the tumor," he said as Jonathan clasped his hands together in delight. He stopped smiling when he noticed the doctor wasn't finished talking.

"Sir, we found several large tumors while your wife was in surgery. I'm afraid that the cancer has spread," he said in a matter of fact tone. Jonathan felt like he had been sucker punched. "So what are you saying," he asked holding on to the pink leather chair in the waiting room to steady himself.

"I would like to see Kelly back in my office as soon as possible so we can discuss the next steps," he advised. "Does… Kelly know," he faltered as his breath caught in his throat. His voice was betraying him, peeling back the curtain on his emotions as a tear trickled down his cheek.

The emphatic doctor placed a hand on Jonathan's shoulder. "Yes, I told her when she came out of surgery. She is a strong woman…wouldn't let me out of her sight until I told her something," he said shaking his head. "Her first words out of surgery were, *did you get it all?*," he imitated Kelly, assuring Jonathan. "She's a fighter," he asserted as Jonathan agreed.

Kelly's surgeon gave Jonathan another pat on the back and retreated from the waiting area. Jonathan sat down in the uncomfortable pink chair and quietly reflected. Here he was doing what he thought was the will of God. He thought that if he did everything that he was supposed to do, share his story, pray and teach the word of God to his family that everything would be fine. How could his wife be going through this right now?

Their bills were piling up and his own strength was wavering. Jonathan didn't know if he could hold it together long enough to keep the strained look of worry from his face. He didn't want to upset his family, but they were in a crisis. His work schedule had become erratic and it resulted in a much lower pay.

He didn't want to admit it but he was beginning to feel like Job, the Biblical figure who endured trials and tribulations to test his faith. A once man of favor, Job lost everything including his children and his livelihood. Through it all, he never lost his faith in God. He was God's example of a person with sound faith.

Jonathan didn't know if he had what it took to endure this situation without fear.

He didn't want to question God's plan but the moment he saw his wife's tiny body lying in the hospital bed he burst into tears. He had no choice but to question everything, now that he was in the position of losing it all.

Luke 8:39

"Return to thine own house, and shew how great things God hath done unto thee. And he went his way, and published throughout the whole city how great things Jesus had done unto him."

Chapter 39

Robert Wellington glanced out of of the large airport windows and exhaled. He tried to quietly reflect as the noise from bustling Amsterdam Airport Schiphol crowded his senses. Five countries in four months, he was exhausted.

He was touring and lecturing around Europe talking about his recent discovery in Egypt and new archeology techniques.

He watched as the room full of eager archeologists mirrored himself, twenty years ago. It seemed like eons ago, but before he lost his best friend, Robert had dreams and hopes that he was sure he'd attain. While he met all of his goals, he didn't have the one person he planned to have with him in the field, Brad.

When they first started planning their archeological expeditions in the Middle East, Brad and Robert felt invincible. Nothing could have stopped them from locating artifacts and evidence that would have put their names in lights. With Brad's dazzling smile and charisma coupled with their undying thirst for knowledge, they were seen as pioneers in their field.

Everyone believed in them.

It still amazed Robert, how quickly life could change.

He and Brad were fresh out of college and eager to test the bounds of archeology with their theories. Twenty years later, he was no longer the student but the teacher in the archeology world. Robert was proud of his accomplishments, but he still felt a profound emptiness.

Over three decades had passed since Robert set out on his first archeological expedition, and while nothing had changed with his hunger for digging up the unknown hadn't changed, his goals had. He was returning home from an expedition in Cairo, Egypt when a family of three sat across from him on the plane.

A young couple, wearing energetic and eager smiles; they appeared to be in their own world. Robert was especially interested in their young child. A chunky little toddler with a head full of chocolate curls, he looked to be delighted with life. He sat on his mother's lap staring in wonder at everything around him.

The entire scene uplifted Robert's spirits.

Robert couldn't take his attention away from the family. He watched as the mother, dressed in traditional clothing held on to her child gently kissing his forehead. The child appeared to be around three years of age, lost in his own world of happiness, as he giggled and laughed with his father. Robert watched as the gentleman kissed his son and wrapped his arms around his wife.

Robert felt a serious pang of loneliness. For the first time in a long time, Robert realized that something was seriously missing from his life.

He needed fellowship with likeminded people. Surprisingly it wasn't easy to find like minded people to vibe with in the field of archeology and science. Robert couldn't wait to return home. He planned to attend service at the Living Waters Baptist Church. He figured visiting Pastor Luke would be healing for him. Simply being in the company of loved ones and family would be enough to lift Robert from his solemn depression.

Growing up as an only child, Robert was accustomed to being alone. His father was also an archeologist, who spent a great deal of his time on the road. Robert was raised almost exclusively by his mother, Fern. Fern was an amazing mother, who made up for his father's absences with love, dedication and attention.

When his father, Edward, returned from his expeditions, he was distant and didn't seem to be comfortable around his family. The few times that Edward Wellington had time for his son, he shared tales of his expeditions and pictures of artifacts. Robert was hooked on the excitement of it all.

He couldn't wait to set out on his own expedition. When he told his father of his plans, the smile on his father's face widened with pride. "My biggest accomplishment is you son," his father said with a pat on his head.

Although he and his father didn't share many heart to heart conversations, Robert never forgot that exchange with his father. His father went on many more expeditions after that, leaving Robert and his mother alone.

Robert learned to find solace in his quiet time.

He enjoyed his alone time, he felt sorry for his colleagues who were away from their families for months at a time. He saw the look of anguish on their faces when they talked to their families at home. Robert affirmed that he would never put a family through the pain of constant goodbyes. As the years dragged on he realized that the comfort of a family, a wife and child to return home to after his long expeditions would be a welcome sight.

For the first time in his life, Robert admitted that he wanted what his friend Brad had.

Robert was ready for a family.

2 Timothy 1:7

"For God hath not given us the spirit of fear; but of power, and of love, and of a sound mind."

Chapter 40

Kelly and Jonathan entered the 10 story brick building through the glass doors and greeted the receptionist at the front desk. The petite woman with a Puerto Rican accent waved at her. "How are you feeling today, Ms. Flannigan?," she asked Kelly with a soothing smile.

"Nervous," Kelly confessed as the receptionist pointed to the scripture on her desk. 2 Timothy 1:7 – "For God has not given us a spirit of fear, but of power, of love and of a sound mind," the scripture read. Kelly recited the words from the scripture considering the words. *If God didn't give her a spirit of fear, then who did?*

She felt Jonathan's hand on her back as he escorted her back to the doctor's office. Dr. Quelo was her new oncologist. He was added to her care team after her surgery. He was the physician who would handle her treatments.

She wasn't looking forward to radiation but she was willing to do anything for the sake of her family. She wanted to live for her daughters and her husband's sake. They wouldn't know how to survive without her. She didn't want to consider the possibility as she took her place on the examination table and held her breath waiting for the doctor to enter the room.

Jonathan stood and placed a hand on his wife's forehead, saying a prayer. Jonathan was used to petitioning God for help. He had been praying for months since he heard about his wife's diagnosis. Jonathon couldn't imagine losing Kelly. She was his backbone. She took care of their children and him with ease. He couldn't do her job even if he tried.

If he lost his wife, Jonathan wasn't sure that he would be able to continue on. He closed his eyes and pleaded with God for good news. Kelly deserved to hear something optimistic after all that she had endured.

While Jonathan prayed for healing, he also knew that he had no real control over his wife's life. Although he wanted to keep her by his side, it was ultimately God's choice and that realization made his eyes water with sadness. He prayed for wisdom and understanding for them both. Most importantly he prayed that his wife's life would be spared. That the doctor would have wonderful news about her condition.

His hopes were shattered when he saw the doctor's face. There was something about the demeanor of his wife's doctor that told Jonathan all he needed to know. Dr. Quelo looked like he wanted to bolt out of the room the moment he entered.

He quietly walked inside the room and clasped his hands together. After considering the possibility, he thought against it and shook Kelly and Jonathan's hands as an exasperated sigh escaped his lips.

"The cancer is out of remission as you both are well aware.," he said shaking his head sadly. "What about radiation, chemotherapy," Kelly asked as he shook his head in disdain. Jonathan could see that the young doctor was wrestling with his response to Kelly. Somehow he could feel the anguish on the doctor.

Dr. Quelo took Kelly's hands in his and squeezed tightly. Jonathan held in his breath trying not to weep openly.

"Kelly, I'm going to level with you, the cancer has spread throughout your body. It's metastasized at such a rate that I'm going to immediately start treatment but I'm not sure if it will be very successful," he said sadly.

"So what are you saying?," Jonathan asked as tears fell. He already knew the answer to his question, but something inside of him had to physically hear it being said. "The cancer is very aggressive," he began as Kelly sobbed softly.

"How long do I have," she asked her doctor frankly. That was Kelly's nature she had to know the answer. There was no point in beating around the bush. She read her results on her surgeon's face the day of her surgery and she could hear the words that her doctor was trying to say. He was telling Kelly that she was dying.

Zephaniah 3:17

"The Lord thy God in the midst of thee is mighty; he will save, he will rejoice over thee with joy; he will rest in his love, he will joy over thee with singing."

Chapter 41

Angela rested at the table and considered the words that Charles conveyed to her. He and his wife raised four of their grandchildren from birth to adulthood. Their son was a drug addict and sadly he couldn't raise his own children. Their mother wasn't capable of doing it because of her raging drug habit, so Charles and his wife Esther decided to take the children and give them a loving, stable home environment.

They raised all successful adults.

He was grateful for the relationship that he fostered with his grandchildren. Each of them helped to check on him and care for him since his wife passed away.

He opened up his heart and poured himself out to Angela and she was enthralled. He was an excellent listener and he understood the grief of losing the love of his life. She explained how she and Brad met in high school and fell in love after being friends for years.

She told him that Brad died when their life was just seeming to get started. Their dream was to live together forever, caring for their grandchildren and sailing around the Caribbean sea sunning all day.

That was the plan but God had a way of making his own plans prevail.

She and Charles had been dating for several weeks after they met in art class. They shared plenty of laughs over coffee after class. Angela couldn't help herself. He was funny, charming and most importantly he was devoted to his walk with Christ.

Charles attended a church 20 miles east of their church. He said that he enjoyed it and felt welcome there. Although Angela wanted him to visit Living Waters Baptist Church she decided to wait a while before suggesting that they visit each other's churches.

They weren't necessarily an item so she didn't want to feed any rumor mills. Their friendship was just blooming and they both made a deal that they would enjoy every second of their relationship.

The phone calls began quite innocently. He called her to check on her when she missed a class due to the flu. She assured him that she was fine and several days later when she returned to class there was a bouquet of white roses on her desk without a card.

She knew who sent it, but Angela didn't know what to do about Charles.

In her years after her husband's death she refused to entertain the idea of dating again, but after her son moved away and started a family of his own she changed her tune. Loneliness was a real thing. After experiencing a profound and deep love with Brad she couldn't wait for her heart to feel something other than grief, again.

She had no choice. It was either, remain stoic and lonely or get out there and enjoy her life. Starting the new class and meeting Edna and Charles helped her realize that there was so much more life out there waiting for her to enjoy.

Isaiah 12:4

"And in that day shall ye say, Praise the Lord, call upon his name, declare his doings among the people, make mention that his name is exalted."

Chapter 42

His workload had increased but that didn't stop Jonathan from putting in the hours to make it all happen. He was exhausted, but he was willing to do what was necessary for his family. That was the least that he could do.

Jonathan knew that soon he would have a decision to make. He located a place that was running a clinical trial for a new drug and Kelly received her approval two days later. He knew that he couldn't possibly take another leave of absence from work and expect them not to fire him.

He considered packing up his family and moving, but he didn't want the move to endanger Kelly since her immune system was weakened due to her treatments. He knew that he had to do something. Holding the letter of resignation in his hand he said a prayer for strength.

Jonathan found strength in watching his wife attend her chemotherapy treatments, faithfully. She took her vitamins and medications without a complaint. When she felt up to it, she and Jonathan went for long strolls through their tree lined neighborhood. They didn't know what the future would hold for their family, but they were willing to go the extra mile together.

When her team informed her of their next approach, Jonathan was relieved to find out that they were stopping the chemotherapy. He witnessed her energy waning and it was heartbreaking. He didn't want her to be on such strong medication and she didn't want it either. It was taking, what little energy she had, away.

They decided on the clinical trial and prayed. God came through in a major way. Jonathan took the letter from his printer tray and walked to his supervisor's office. "Bob, can I talk to you for a moment?," he asked as he walked inside and handed Bob his resignation letter.

Bob worked as the managing attorney for their legal team. He made the final decisions that went to Human Resources and was considered, their Boss. Jonathan rarely spoke to him because Bob made it known that he wasn't interested in friendship or teamwork for that matter. In their office it was every man for himself. Jonathan took a deep breath and prepared for that day to be his last in the division.

He was shocked to hear that Bob wouldn't accept the letter of resignation. Bob asked Jonathan to apply for FMLA for his wife's care and to see what the firm did after that. He reminded Jonathan that with Kelly being ill the last thing he needed was to completely resign from his position.

Jonathan was blessed to have a supervisor who cared enough to look out for him, but he'd already made up his mind. While he withdrew his resignation letter his decision was made, they were moving to Minnesota.

When he walked inside the house he let out a sigh of relief. The smell of freshly baked bread and the sounds of laughter were intoxicating. Brittany's giggles permeated the air like laughing gas. The two girls were playing with balloons yelling with glee.

Jonathan felt like a weight was lifted from his shoulders the moment he made the decision to pack up and move with his family across the country. His wife would have a chance to heal in peace and his daughters would benefit from the extra attention his grandfather and mother would surely show them.

Brittany bounced around the house with full energy and kept her sister occupied. For the most part, aside from her treatment days and overall lack of energy, Kelly maintained her obligations with a joyfulness. She was happy to get out of bed and dress the girls for daycare. Jonathan finally convinced her to take a leave of absence from her job so she spent her days relaxing at home.

One of their neighbors, Debra was in the kitchen, busying herself preparing dinner. Debra was a blessing to their family. She prepared meals for their family and cleaned their home twice per month.

Although Jonathan and Kelly paid her for the cleaning and catering services; Debra infused care and love into everything she did. It felt like they had a mother popping in every so often. For that they both were grateful.

The clinical trial was being hosted at the Maplewood Cancer Center in Minnesota. The center was precisely six miles from Angela's home in Maple Grove. Jonathan was looking forward to being in close proximity to his mother. He needed her strength and wisdom more than anything.

1 Peter 1:8

"Whom having not seen, ye love; in whom, though now ye see him not, yet believing, ye rejoice with joy unspeakable and full of glory."

Chapter 43

Angela flitted about the apartment tidying up the place, preparing for Jonathan and Kelly's visit. She had fresh flowers cut and placed in just about every corner she could find. Jonathan drove his family from New York City to Minnesota.

They broke up the 19 hour drive into three days and took the scenic route. He called and checked in with her at every stopping point. The girls seemed to enjoy the traveling and to his delight, Kelly did too. Everyone was looking forward to their new life in Minnesota, including Angela.

She found them a two bedroom apartment in Maplewood. It was only five minutes away from the facility where Kelly was being treated. Angela planned to take care of the girls on the days that Kelly received treatment. She would stay at her house with them so Jonathan and Kelly could both rest.

Angela welcomed the company.

She wasn't lonely thanks to Charles who was attached to her hip, but she wouldn't have had it any other way. After their art class ended, they signed up for hand dancing and a basic introduction to computing course. They planned to make their life one of learning and traveling.

Her life was so much richer now that she met Charles. They went ice fishing together and skiing at Gooseberry Falls. Angela and Charles went on dates that required hiking boots, and camping gear. She felt like a teenager all over again. It was invigorating.

Angela's cell phone rang loudly on the mantle. She glided over to the phone expecting it to be Charles, to her surprise it was Anna. She loved talking to Anna and she missed her. Since she started dating Charles her and Anna scaled back their, "girl's night in" to every once in a while instead of the usual monthly schedule.

"Hi Sweetie," she said as Anna smiled at the sound of her voice. "Hey, what are you doing?," she asked as Angela informed her that she was in Jonathan's new place waiting on them to arrive. "Oh," Anna said as her voice trailed off. "I'm praying for all of you, Angela. I'm so sorry that Kelly has to go through this," she said sadly.

"Please give them my best when you talk to them," she offered as she quickly ended the phone call. Angela hung up the phone and continued working on the girl's room. She wanted it to be welcoming when they came home.

Angela was still in the room that resembled a pink explosion when Jonathan and Kelly walked inside. They both were overjoyed about the decorations and how homey she made the apartment for their arrival. "Thank you so much," Kelly cooed as she looked around. "This is beautiful," she said smelling the white roses on the table as her eyes lit up.

"I think there are flowers in every room," she exclaimed with an innocent joy, which warmed Angela's heart. Kelly's face was bright with enthusiasm as Jonathan shot her a look of pure gratitude. Her mission was accomplished. After she gave them all hugs she kissed her sleeping granddaughters and left them to explore their new home.

John 16:24

"Hitherto have ye asked nothing in my name: ask, and ye shall receive, that your joy may be full."

Chapter 44

Anna dressed and prepared for her day at the school. She was ready to take on another new week and couldn't wait to implement her lesson plans with the little ones. They were going to make a rubber egg using nothing but vinegar and an ordinary egg. She smiled to herself as she imagined the looks of shock when she shined the flashlight on the rubber egg.

In her twenty years of teaching that was one of her favorite science experiments. Anna was unashamed to admit that she enjoyed the project more than the kids. Anna loved her job. She didn't have to set an alarm at night, her passion for the students had her up on time every morning.

When she skipped through the doors of the school she walked straight to her classroom and prepped for the experiment. It would be the first task of the day.

Her students began flowing into the classroom as she sipped on her tea waiting for the classroom to fill up with eager little faces. As soon as the bell rang she sprung into action. "Guess what day it is?" she asked as the deafening screams made her jump, "Rubber Egg Day," they yelled as she laughed.

Suddenly there was a knock at her classroom door. She sighed feeling terrible about the noise. Figuring it was a teacher who her class undoubtedly disturbed she opened the door with an apology on her lips.

Instead she came face to face with the love of her life.

As her face flushed red, she took a step back and smiled, "Jonathan, what brings you here," she asked as he walked into the classroom with two little girls holding on to his hand for dear life.

"This is Brittany and Brianna. They would like to join your class," Jonathan announced trying to pry the girls off of him so they could meet their teacher. "Girls do you remember me," she asked as she leaned down closer to them and looked in their eyes. When they looked at her their eyes widened with recognition.

Jonathan was shocked and relieved to see his girls take their seats and involve themselves in the rubber egg experiment. When he was satisfied that they were comfortable he snuck out of the room and left them in Anna's capable hands.

When he reached the Maplewood Cancer Center, Kelly was there waiting for him. She had already been through the triage process and was hooked up to the machines receiving what they hoped was a life saving solution, intravenously. Kelly looked so small in the bed. She appeared childlike to him. Jonathan's heart broke a little every time he was near his wife, but he couldn't spend a moment away from her without a profound aching in his chest.

As usual, Kelly didn't care about what she had going on, she was worried about the girls. "How are the girls doing," she strained to speak. He leaned over and placed a loving kiss on her forehead. Her breathing was heavy and erratic, like every breath took monumental effort.

Being this close to her, watching the love of his life experience agony, made him feel utterly powerless. He wiped a tear away before she noticed and cleared his throat. "They're fine. I just got them settled in school," he said with a strained smile. "Everything will be just fine now," Jonathan assured as he watched his wife drift off to sleep.

Matthew 18:19

"Again I say unto you, That if two of you shall agree on earth as touching any thing that they shall ask, it shall be done for them of my Father which is in heaven."

Chapter 45

Pastor Luke lead the congregation in prayer as Jonathan subconsciously checked out, half listening. His mind wasn't on church, it was in Maplewood where his wife was struggling to survive. His mother and daughters sat next to him keeping him company as his grandfather delivered a fiery sermon. Angela had become his rock, she gave his hand a firm squeeze every so often to remind him that she was right there.

His faith was waning and they both knew it.

Churches from across the world had contacted him trying to book him for their revival services and events. They wanted him to share his testimony with their congregation. He had to admit that his testimony was powerful enough to make people stop and consider the possibility of life without God. It was terrifying enough to make nonbelievers cry out, "What can I do to be saved?"

He didn't feel the same anymore. His wife was fighting the toughest battle in her life, his daughters were facing a life without their mother and he was mentally wasted. He couldn't paste a smile on his face and pretend like everything was alright.

Instead, he simply ignored the calls. How could he encourage anyone while his life was in shambles? It just didn't seem right. Could he give praises to God while suffering from His delayed response to Jonathan's prayers.

He trusted that God would heal his wife, but she was deteriorating right before his eyes. She was declining so swiftly he had to prepare himself to see her every time he visited her. She was so faithful, even in her worst state she smiled when he read her scriptures and prayed for her.

Their love for each other deepened as they faced Kelly's mortality together. Jonathan was scared, for the second time in his life he was losing someone who meant the world to him. How would he go on without Kelly? He had been asking himself that same question for months, but at that moment he knew that he had to face the reality. He may just lose his wife.

His grandfather asked him to say a few words for the church and he couldn't bring himself to do it. How could he? How could he motivate other people when he was feeling so low down himself? He couldn't do it, so he didn't even try.

He began to resent the time that he spent sharing his testimony. He could've spent that time with his wife. Had he known that this could be the end, he would have done things differently.

He was devastated.

After service Jonathan's mother took the girls to the event hall for ice cream and cake. She promised to bring them back to the apartment later that evening but she wanted her son to get some rest in between that time.

As she walked off Jonathan stood in the hallway feeling lost. He must've looked lost as well because he could hear chuckling behind him. He turned to face Anna who smiled, "are you lost," she teased as his face crumbled in a sea of tears.

Anna didn't know what to do, she didn't want to upset Jonathan she was only joking with Jonathan. Anna walked him to an empty classroom and closed the door. She hugged Jonathan, rubbing his back as he cried on her shoulder. "I'm so sorry Jonathan," she said as she began to pray for her friend.

She didn't have to ask him what was wrong. She already knew it in her heart. Jonathan was losing his best friend. When he finally stopped crying, she offered him a tissue and a smile. "You needed to get that out," she said before he could fix his mouth to say, sorry.

He thanked her as she headed to the door. "Everything will be alright Jonathan. Trust God," she said as he broke down crying. "How can I trust him? He's taking my wife away from me. I did what he wanted me to do and he's taking Kelly," he whined as tears fell freely.

"Jonathan, we are not that powerful. We don't know what God's plans are and sometimes we are left with nothing but questions. Those are the times when you need to really trust God to have your back. You can't lean to your own understanding. That will get you every single time. We are human, our understanding is flawed," she continued to encourage Jonathan as he dried his tears.

He talked to Anna for over an hour in the classroom, pouring out his heart. It felt good to be understood. He spent plenty of time talking to his therapist about Kelly and his fears about losing her only to be told to grow from love and to learn to love. He didn't even know what she was talking about.

All his friend needed to hear was his tears and she understood. On his drive to Maplewood he considered just how blessed he really was. God was giving him just what he needed to make it through this time in his life and He would continue to keep them.

He just needed to keep the faith.

Matthew 5:4

"Blessed are they that mourn: for they shall be comforted."

Chapter 46

If you would have asked anyone in town who had a chance to get to know them, they would have told you that Kelly Klein was loved by everyone but no one loved her like her husband. On the day Kelly died, Jonathan wept like never before. He felt completely hollow inside. Angela moved Jonathan and the girls to her home so she could care for them there.

Although it wasn't the most ideal situation, she basked in the glory of being a full time grandmother. She took her granddaughters on nature trail walks, to the library and to different community events in an effort to get their mind off of the unrelenting sadness that they all felt.

Kelly was a treasured soul and she touched so many others during her time on earth. It moved her tremendously to see that her entire family showed up to her funeral in droves. She had never met any of Kelly's siblings but when she posted Kelly's obituary on Facebook a surprising thing happened.

Angela received an "instant message" from someone named Christopher Klein. Angela didn't ordinarily use Facebook, but Anna helped her log in and access the message. When they saw the name, Klein they were both intrigued. Christopher was Kelly's nephew, one of 32 children born from her many siblings.

According to Christopher they believed that Kelly was missing for nearly twenty years. The family hired private investigators to locate Kelly but could never find her, until they saw Angela's message. Christopher messaged her with such enthusiasm that Angela couldn't help herself.

Although, she never mentioned her family, Angela felt that it was only right that they have the opportunity to pay their last respects. She didn't expect, the entire family to show up, however.

She and Jonathan had the chance to meet all twelve of Kelly's siblings and all 32 of her nieces and nephews. Brianna and Brittany were delighted to know that they had so many cousins. It was a beautiful moment to witness.

It hurt Angela to realize that so much was going on around them, yet Jonathan was too depressed to make it out of the bed most days. She knew that feeling all too well but tried her best not to rush his progress, but she was growing increasingly concerned about his mental wellbeing.

Several months passed and Jonathan hadn't made any progress. She didn't want to rush his grieving, but she also knew how quickly grief could spiral into depression and her son couldn't afford that. He had an entire family counting on him.

Angela remembered the feeling of losing a loved one suddenly. It hurt her deeply to see her son going through what she'd experienced nearly two decades prior. Kelly was such a sweet soul, she often wondered about the beautiful spirits that left the world too soon.

Jonathan tried to get himself together after her death for the sake of his daughters, but he suffered from a devastating bout of depression. She listened to her son talk, she encouraged him but she felt herself slipping into her own depression by simply witnessing what her son endured.

He drifted in and out of despair, choosing to remain in his room for the majority of the day. Jonathan slept all night. His daughters barely had time with him. When he wasn't closed up inside the bedroom, Angela found her son sitting outside staring at nothing. She could feel Jonathan's pain and it broke her heart to see how his emptions affected her granddaughters. While they missed their mother, they couldn't understand why their father had suddenly changed.

These were the times when she missed her husband the most. Brad would have known exactly what to say and do to snap Jonathan out of his depression. Her husband, Brad would listen to his son vent and then advise him in a way that Jonathan truly believed he came up with an idea organically. Angela knew that she didn't possess that same power of persuasion over her son.

She just wanted him to snap out of it, but she knew personally how grief had a way of grabbing ahold of someone and never letting go. She wanted more for Jonathan than a life of grief. It took her years to recover from losing her husband, Brad. Angela learned in the process that she had to relinquish the illusion of control. Once she surrendered her grief and control over her own life's plans she saw her pain ease.

She refused to be hard on her son, but Angela was determined not to let Jonathan sink too far in the pit of despair. Angela understood how he was feeling so she tried her best to help her son see the positive side to life, but nothing seemed to bring the light back in his eyes.

"Desperate times call for desperate measures," she said determined to break her son out of the prison of hopelessness. Holding the phone in her hand she took a deep breath as the phone rang. "Hey Anna, I need a favor," she pleaded as soon as Anna answered the phone.

Nehemiah 8:10

"Do not grieve, for the joy of the Lord is your strength."

Chapter 47

Anna gazed lovingly into Jonathan's bloodshot eyes, taking in his disheveled appearance and unshaven face broke her heart. She wanted to say something or do something to bring back the Jonathan that she once knew. The fun-loving, ever smiling friend. Instead, she saw a complete shell of a person when she looked at her friend. She was determined to change that.

Swirling the straw absently in his large chocolate milkshake, Jonathan struggled to pay attention. Everything seemed to distract his attentiveness. Jonathan didn't know whether he was coming or going, but he knew one thing that he couldn't continue to go on like this.

"So, a rabbit and a frog walk into a bar, and the bartender goes, "Hey we have a drink named after you," she said chuckling before she could get the joke out. "And the frog said, "You... have a drink named...Phil?" Anna amused as Jonathan stared at her in disbelief before laughing hysterically.

"That was the worst joke I've ever heard," he said laughing uncontrollably. After they recovered, he smiled at his friend. It had been so long since he had a real laugh. He wanted to thank her, but he could tell that the laughter they shared was thanks enough.

"You were always terrible at telling jokes," he said chuckling.

Anna smiled, her mission had been accomplished. She knew that a horrible joke would be the best ice breaker. He was never one to let a lousy joke go without saying something. She loved that about him.

Jonathan drove to Angela's house wearing a smile for the first time in weeks. He and Anna reminisced about their time in high school. During their youth, they were quite rebellious for a time, but they also found a way to have fun and enjoy each others company. When Brad Flannigan died, Anna became Jonathan's lifeline. While, they found themselves in trouble, several times, Anna and Jonathan were a great comfort to each other.

When they arrived at Angela's house, Jonathan was surprised to see a red Chrysler Sebring parked in the driveway. Curiously, he stared at the license plates, trying to give himself a clue about his mother's mysterious visitor. "Who's visiting?" Anna asked as he held her car door open. Jonathan couldn't help but chuckle at her question.

They were both overprotective of Angela. It gave Jonathan a sense of peace to know that Anna loved his mother as if she were his own. He needed that reassurance that if something happened to him, his mother was taken care of.

He reached inside his pocket and pulled out the note. The note was alarming but straightforward. It read only four words, "Go HOME or ELSE." Jonathan knew what they were referring to. He had been receiving threats since they arrived in Minnesota. Although the arrival of the first letter was a shock to Jonathan, he didn't tell anyone, not even his grandfather.

The day after his powerful testimony, Jonathan received the first letter. He found it after the church service, jammed inside his drivers' side window. Someone wasn't happy about the fact that he was sharing his testimony with the masses, but that didn't stop Jonathan.

He was sure that the same person sending him letters was behind his tires being slashed in the rental car, twice. Jonathan didn't worry about it, he just reported the vandalism and continued to minister the Gospel.

When they opened the front door of his childhood home, Jonathan and Anna were met with the decadent smell of baked cookies. "We're in here," Angela called from the living room as he walked inside the home and grabbed three cookies from the cooling rack. Anna bypassed the cookies and went directly to the living room to check on Angela.

She smiled at the smartly dressed gentleman seated across from Angela on the sofa. His handsome face wore a bright smile as he offered his hand towards Anna. "Anna, this is our friend Robert Wellington," Angela said as she introduced Anna and Robert. "Hey, how are you doing?" Anna asked as she shook his hand with a smile. Anna greeted Angela with a hug and a kiss on the cheek.

Jonathan walked inside the living room with his mouth filled with cookies as Angela chuckled. "Jonathan you remember Dr. Wellington," she said as Jonathan hurried across the room and embraced Robert in a brotherly hug. Angela watched as the two men talked excitedly. "You look great, man. What have you been up to?" Jonathan asked as Robert shook his head sadly. "Nothing much. I just wanted to get away from it all and disconnect for a while. I figured I'd stop in and check on your family," he said as Jonathan nodded his understanding.

"I'm sorry to hear about your wife," Robert remarked sadly. "Thank you, man," Jonathan responded as an uncomfortable silence covered the room like a thick fog. "Anna, can you help me in the kitchen? I was just about to prepare the sides for dinner. Robert, would you please join us for dinner?" she asked as Robert smiled. "Of course. You won't be getting rid of me that quickly," he responded.

Anna followed Angela in the kitchen and busied herself with the meal preparation as the two men caught up with each other. "How was your day?" Angela asked. Anna paused for a moment from slicing cucumbers and considered Angela's loaded question. "Everything went well. Jonathan will be just fine. I think he needs to spend more time out of the house, so I'm going to try my best to get him out to Bible Study tomorrow evening," Anna responded as Angela nodded with a smile.

Angela was grateful for Anna's presence in her life. She always wanted a daughter. She and Brad often talked about expanding their family, but their hopes for more children were dashed when he died.

Although Angela dated, she couldn't see herself in a serious relationship, especially not immediately after Brad's death. Anna came into her life just as Jonathan started his new life in New York City. She stayed by Angela's side and helped ease the pain of loneliness without Jonathan.

Angela smiled at the lovely Anna as she stirred the bubbling pot of spaghetti sauce, intent on preparing a perfect meal for them. Angela said a silent prayer of gratitude for Anna. It didn't take the two determined women long to pull together a meal of spaghetti and meat sauce with garlic bread and salad.

Anna spooned the last of the sauce in the large serving bowl when the doorbell rang. Angela smiled as she walked to the door and opened it for Pastor Luke. "Good evening Angela, thank you for the dinner invite," Pastor Luke said wrapping his arms around Angela in a warm embrace. "Wow, something smells wonderful," Pastor Luke remarked as he made his way into the dining room.

He gasped in amazement when he saw Robert seated at the table. "Surprise!" Angela said with a wide grin. "Look who came to visit," she said as Pastor Luke embraced his friend Robert and offered him a firm pat on the back.

"It's good to see you, son," Pastor Luke said as Robert nodded. "You too, sir," he responded. Robert felt comfort in Luke's presence.

He desperately wanted to pull the wise older gentleman aside and ask him for prayer. The longer Robert remained in the presence of Brad's family, the sadder he grew. Anna and Angela brought the food out to the table as Robert filled Jonathan and Luke in on the latest expedition.

Isaiah 55:12

"For ye shall go out with joy, and be led forth with peace: the mountains and the hills shall break forth before you into singing, and all the trees of the field shall clap their hands."

Chapter 48

Jonathan and Robert sat outside enjoying the warm summer breeze. They discussed the latest find in an excavation within Nepal. Robert was excited about the prospects and eager to get started. He told Jonathan that the project wouldn't begin for another six months. "So, I decided to head home for a while to rest up," Robert explained.

Robert's excitement about the upcoming excavation was contagious. They discussed the preliminaries concerning the project, as Robert showed images of what they hoped to locate. They had maps and guides ready to go. The entire conversation reminded Jonathan of the times he shared with his father. He hadn't seen enthusiasm like this since Brad Flannigan.

Jonathan knew that Robert felt it too because of the long silence that ensued afterward. They both missed Brad. He would have taken over the entire conversation with a joke or a story from the past.

"So, Jonathan how are you?" Robert asked as he turned to face him. "I know that you have been through a great deal recently. How are you holding up?" he asked wearing a look of concern on his face.

"It's been a challenge trying to get back to a place of reality without her," Jonathan said sadly. "I don't know how I'm going to move on without Kelly," Jonathan added as Robert nodded in agreement.

"I'm sorry, man. I can't imagine. I've been praying for you guys since the day I heard about your wife's illness," Robert said. "Pastor Luke has been keeping in contact with me. It feels good to talk to him, you know?" Robert said as Jonathan agreed. "Sometimes, he seems like the only person who can break life down to a Biblical perspective. He sends me right into the scripture no matter my troubles," Robert confessed.

"Yeah, my grandfather has been my lifeline for so long. I don't know if I would have made it through without him, especially with Kelly being sick. He prayed for me and encouraged me. I just wish I could take him back to New York with me," Jonathan added with a chuckle.

"You think you're ready for the full responsibility of the girls and everything without Kelly?" Robert asked. "Not at all," Jonathan admitted. "My mother wouldn't be comfortable with things if I left for New York right now, anyway. She thinks the girls will do better in Minnesota. I haven't been in much of a position to disagree with her, lately," he admitted.

Robert sighed and laid a heavy arm around Jonathan's shoulders. "Take your time, man. Grief lasts for a long time, you have to just give yourself enough time to feel it all and to live through it," Robert added.

"I lost my beloved mother last year, and that's one of the things I've been trying to remind myself of," Robert confessed. "My mother was my only family for over thirty years after my father left us. It broke my heart to bury her. I didn't think that I would ever move beyond the grief until your grandfather called me," he said with a sad chuckle.

"It was as if he knew that I was suffering from an emotional breakdown. Pastor Luke prayed for me before I told him about my mother's death. He told me to feel the grief and acknowledge it. That was the only way I made it through. Your grandfather's advice and prayer," Robert said.

"I know what you mean, Robert. I don't know what I would do without that old man's wisdom," he added. Pastor Luke was the backbone of their family. He kept Jonathan encouraged when he wanted to give up.

After Jonathan said goodnight to Robert, he dialed his grandfather's phone number. "Hey, Young Fella," his grandfather chuckled on the phone. "Hey Old Man," Jonathan teased. "I was just about to call you. I was invited to attend a revival at Greater Faith Ministries in the downtown area. I can't attend. I was wondering if you could go in my place," Pastor Luke asked as Jonathan held the phone in stunned silence.

This would be the first time he spoke to a congregation without Kelly. Was he ready? Things had changed. His mind had changed. He no longer
252

cared about the reception he would receive, Jonathan desperately wanted to accomplish his mission.

He was going to spread the gospel and share with the world how things would be without God. The visions of people celebrating that there was no God in the streets haunted Jonathan. It bothered him because he knew that he played a part in their joys. The visions of rampant sin and lustful desires being fulfilled in the streets were too much for him to bare. Jonathan had to warn them all that they were headed towards certain destruction.

It was his purpose to help people visualize just how badly they needed God's direction and correction in their lives. Jonathan recalled the conversations that he had with the ministers and religious leaders when he showed them the evidence that God didn't exist. He remembered the way his stomach sank as they rejoiced and quickly moved to denounce their religious texts.

Some shocked him, however with their undying faith. At that time Jonathan was determined to erase God from everything. His surprise came when steadfast religious leaders banded together and proclaimed that God existed. They called Jonathan's revelations lies and continued with their worship of God.

Their faith in God never wavered. Even when Priests, Preachers, Mosque Leaders, and Pastors were being burned for proclaiming God's existence, they still held firm. They never bent to the wills of the world.

Jonathan had to recall their resolve when he returned to the pulpit. His sermons and testimonies would no longer tickle the ears of congregants. He would have to expose the revelations that were revealed to him, even if it made others uncomfortable.

Luke could only imagine the look on his grandson's face. Luke knew that it was asking a lot of Jonathan to leave his family and go several hundred miles away to minister, but he also knew that it was a necessity. Jonathan had a mission to accomplish.

As if he was reading Jonathan's mind, his grandfather chimed in, "Son, if you're not ready, it's alright," he said. "There will be more times for you to minister," he said as Jonathan cleared his throat and stuck out his chest.

"No, Pop. I can handle it. It would be an honor for me to do this. Please let them know that I will deliver the sermon in your place," he said. Jonathan wasn't entirely sure that he could handle the engagement, but he refused to let his grandfather or God down.

As the images returned to his mind, Jonathan knew that he had no choice. He had to reach out to the world and warn them. If they didn't get themselves together, things would end badly.

Jonathan was determined to carry out his responsibility. The world was already operating as if God didn't exist, Jonathan had to let them all know what he witnessed with his own eyes.

He was their only hope.

Acts 2:38

"Then Peter said unto them, Repent, and be baptized every one of you in the name of Jesus Christ for the remission of sins, and ye shall receive the gift of the Holy Ghost."

Chapter 49

Jonathan kneeled and began his prayer. He was inside the Preacher's Office at Greater Faith Ministries in downtown Minnesota. The tiny room was decorated in wall to wall wood paneling. Trinkets and crystal angels lined the wall across from him while a picture of Jesus hung on the wall behind him.

Symphonic sounds permeated the air from the choir singing praises below. The church wasn't an immaculately decorated megachurch, but Jonathan was just as grateful to be there.

Jonathan was just happy to be able to spread the gospel at the church. He was determined to do right by not only his grandfather, but by his duties to God. He began to pray before his sermon. Jonathan would not let his fear intimidate him enough to quit his mission. Just as he concluded his conversation with God, he heard a soft knock on the door. "Come in," Jonathan said as he checked his reflection in the mirror.

He smiled at the short, stout man dressed in a tight black suit with a red and white bow tie, standing in front of him. "Pastor Flannigan, we were looking for your biography. Sister Easton plans to read it before we introduce you to the congregation," he said as he clasped his hands in front of Jonathan.

Jonathan reached inside his briefcase and removed the one-page document. He handed the paper to the short man who introduced himself as Brother Tim Johnson.

He tried not to watch the man as he read over the biography with a look of disapproval. "It doesn't say anywhere here that you are the Pastor at Living Waters Baptist Church," he said growing hysterical. "I'm not the Preacher there. I am Pastor Flannigan's grandson. I am here to share my testimony with your congregation," he said as the gentleman took a confused step backward shaking his head disapprovingly.

"Um...I'll be right back," Brother Tim Johnson responded as he scurried out of the room. Jonathan sat down in the overstuffed chair, his emotions reeling. He didn't know what was going to happen next. All he knew was he had an obligation to share his testimony with the world. He had to let everyone know what would happen in a world without a God.

Suddenly, he heard another knock at the door. "Come in," Jonathan responded halfheartedly. He quickly composed himself as the Pastor of the church entered the room. "I am Pastor Ethan Moran. Jonathan, we are so blessed to have you here. You come highly recommended from

Pastor Luke Flannigan. I just wanted to come in and formally introduce myself to you," he said offering his left hand.

The Pastor Moran was a few years older than Jonathan, but he looked very well cared for. He was a fit man with bright green eyes and a full head of red hair. He was dressed smartly in a gray suit. Jonathan could tell by the man's demeanor that he was a man of prestige and honor. The Pastor accompanied Brother Johnson and Jonathan to the sanctuary. Jonathan looked around the large area and let out a deep breath. It was really happening.

"Thank you, God," Jonathan said as he slowly approached the pulpit.

Jonathan walked slowly out on the brightly lit stage to a huge crowd of liberal members that welcomed anyone to become a member of their congregation. Dressed in a conservative pin striped suit, shiny Stacy Adam shoes, white shirt, and Kelly's favorite blue stripped tie, Jonathan turned and nervously faced and smiled at the people whom would receive the full revelation that God placed in his heart.

Jonathan flipped on his note book and paused for a minute to thank God for the opportunity to share God's vision to the people. He slowly opened his eyes and felt the warm bright lights beaming on his face. The crowd starred back anticipating a traditional testimony often given by guest Preachers.

"Back in high school, I couldn't wait for the day to travel around the world discovering historical artifacts that supported the birth, life and death of Jesus Christ with my father Brad Flannigan and my grandfather, Pastor Luke Flannigan. It soon became an nightmare when my Mom received a phone call that would change my life forever, from my grandfather, who was in the Middle East. I heard my Mom scream and I rushed to see what was happening and I saw my Mom kneeling on the floor weeping uncontrollably. The sadness on her face was frightening. My heart began to pound rapidly as she mustered a bit of strength to tell me my father had been killed," Jonathan said as the crowd gasped in sadness.

Wiping away a single tear, Jonathan continued with his testimony, "How could this be? I questioned God! My father gave his entire life proving your very existence and my grandfather preached your love, mercy, and grace at your church every Sunday for over 40 years!" he exclaimed. As he spoke, Jonathan began to relive the anger and pain he felt many years ago. He paused for a moment and then continued.

"This news devastated our family, our church, and our community. Within my heart I could no longer believe in a God that would destroy a God fearing family. I turned my back on God, on my family, and left my home," Jonathan said.

As he reached into his pocket to pull out a handkerchief tears begin to roll down Jonathan's face as the sympathetic crowd focused on every word.

"I became an Atheist. Years later, I received an invitation to go the place where my father died in the Middle East. Unknowing to anyone else I had one goal and that was to prove that there is no God. While I was there I had an unfortunate accident. I fell into one of the dig site's pit. I hit my head during the fall and was unconscious for a period of time. This was when I had a vision from God. He shared with me these revelations," Jonathan said growing excited as he recalled the visions God showed him.

"God revealed to me how Satan was beginning to remove Him from the hearts and minds of his people particularly in the United States. God chose this land, this Gentile country to be the people to spread the Gospel of His Son Jesus Christ around the world. Satan has begun to raise up! He's using anti-Christ disciples to remove God from the schools, public places and political buildings around this country. Christ is and has been the foundation of our country from the beginning. Satan was using the media (television, radio, newspaper, FB, Twitter, Instagram, etc.) to promote a liberal and free society, and unrestricted life style. If Satan is successful in removing God from the hearts and minds of His people it would be easy for Satan to shift the moral compass of our nation," He advised as the members in the congregation nodded and murmured their agreement with his words.

"We as a people will begin to believe that all of our great accomplishments, that our nation's power and authority, our prosperity, wealth, and success was all achieved without God. The United States is blessed and anointed by God, for God's purpose. We all are blessed to had been born here and live here for a time such as this. Satan wants us to believe that there is no God and we don't need a God. When I was unconscious in that pit, God allowed me to see what the world would be like if there was No God," Jonathan said wiping away the sweat from his brow with his handkerchief. He watched as the congregation's eyes were glued on him, waiting to hear the rest of his testimony with baited breath.

"That was my goal as an Atheist and so, God allowed me to experience a life without God in that revelation. I believed that I had found proof from a secret and ancient library full of religious books. Hidden from mankind because these ancient books proved that man wrote these books to put restraints, limitations, and control over man. Man realized centuries ago that if the masses didn't believe that there was life after death, he would be held accountable for his "sin" he would eventually destroy himself. These books would prove that there was no God. Finally, I found what I was looking for. I took those books and shared it with the entire world," Jonathan continued.

"I saw in my revelation that I gained worldwide fame and recognition, power, wealth and success and the world applauded me for the findings. The world celebrated and embraced a world without God," he said as everyone smiled at his vision.

"As time went on the world rapidly began to change. People had lost or set aside their moral compass and the Christian foundation that gave them hope and peace. They had no reason to restrain themselves from their every thought, imagination and every action. They no longer had an accountability or feared being held accountable for lying, cheating, being dishonest, hateful actions, disloyalty, and sin in general after death. There was no Heaven nor Hell. You live and you died. There was no life after death that would hold you accountable for your sin," Jonathan said as he watched the congregation's reaction to his words. He noticed that some members were shifting in their seats, but a few had their eyes locked on his. They were listening.

"The Church would become luke-warm, watering down God's message about the Gospel. Mega Churches would rise throughout the country, led by Pastor's that were not called into the ministry. They will use the church as a platform for power, greed, prosperity and fame. Preaching without any supporting scriptures or revelations from God. They desire to be served and not servants. They desire the attention and acceptance of big business, politicians, and other famous people. They will compromise their ministry for wealth, fame, and recognition. The world became a dog eat dog world. A world where churches were burned and crumbled. Preachers were jailed and persecuted. People felt they were betrayed," Jonathan expressed with excitement as he continued explaining his visions.

"Since there was no God, men and women began to divorce at an alarming rate. Adultery became a common practice. The sexual revolution exploded. Women were abused and rape crimes became common place. Homosexuality became as an acceptable behavior and same sex marriages exploded in all the communities. Law enforcement were out manned and could not contain nor control crimes in their communities. The movies, sports, and entertainment would replace God on Sundays. The movies would began to shape the hearts and minds of our society with sex, violence, crime, and include God's name, the church language, and the Christian values to cause doubt, confusion, disbelief, or simply either label it as old fashions or a myth," Jonathan explained as he watched some members in the congregation shift uncomfortably in their seats.

"Even the Christian community were consuming themselves with sports on Sundays. And now they are consumed throughout the entire week spending billions of dollars on sporting events and neglecting the church and their families. The federal government was consumed by lying politicians seeking power for their own personal interests. They governed for special interested groups. Politicians would pass laws in favor of those who assisted with keeping them in office and in power. They no longer hold tech companies and other big business accountable to the consumers," Jonathan said.

"Greed and power would become the addiction for the wealthy. The Food and Drug Industry plotted how they could earn trillions of dollars by reducing the availability of healthy and nutritious foods and ingredients from the food supply. They made it difficult for the poor to have access to local grocery stores to purchase basic needs," Jonathan advised as he heard groans from the audience, he continued to speak.

"Farmers and business owners raised the cost for organic foods so that only the middle and upper class could afford it. Soon they will privatize the water supply and what was one time a public service directly to our homes we will have pay for it by the bottle. The lack of nutritious foods, vitamins, and other healthy ingredients would create a society of people with minor illnesses such as high blood pressure, diabetics, sleep apnea, high cholesterol and other life threatening illness such as cancer. Their goal was to make sure every human being became dependent on some kind of drug or medication. Even the poor had access to drugs whereby they could suppress their stress and pain. The federal government made the use of marijuana, legal," he said staring out at the underwhelmed audience.

"As God continued to reveal to me what was happening around the world and how mankind was destroying His greatest creation I began to realize the huge mistake I made by sharing with the world that there was no God. I hated what I had done and decided to end it all. Yes, I jumped out of a luxury high rise apartment. As I fell to end it all I heard God's voice call me and at that time I woke up from the pit knowing that God gave be the burden to warn the world we were creating and that

Satan is gaining momentum," Jonathan concluded wiping his sweaty brow with the damp handkerchief. His heart pounded with intensity as he placed the wireless microphone on the pulpit and stepped back, staring at the congregation.

The liberal congregation was in shock. They couldn't believe Jonathan's testimony. They wondered how could he be so negative about the world when everything was so wonderful. They felt that he had condemned everything they thought was wonderful and good.

As he concluded his testimony and scanned the reaction of his audience he could tell that it was not well received. The Pastor walked out on the stage and offered a modest applause and quickly escorted Jonathan to his office. The Pastor was also disappointed about Jonathan's sermon. Not only did he feel it was inappropriate, it hit too close to home.

Without knowing, most of the things Jonathan shared with them pointed directed at the Pastor and it revealed the luke-warm messages the congregation had received Sunday after Sunday. His congregation was not prepared to hear a message that cut at the core of their ministry.

The Pastor harshly asked Jonathan to leave. But Jonathan was beaming and wanted to continue to share his revelation to anyone who would listen.

As he stepped out into the warm air, he felt can exuberance like none other. The fire inside of him burned red-hot with furor. Jonathan was compelled to tell someone about his visions. He stood on the street and called out to anyone who would listen. "Have you ever wondered what would happen to the world if there was no God?" he asked as people looked at him like he was crazy.

"Let me tell you what happened to me...," Jonathan said as he began to explain to the passersby about God. He felt helpless as people laughed at him and called him crazy. "I'm not crazy!" he yelled. People walking down the street looked at him and crossed the street in an attempt to get away from him.

No one wanted to hear what Jonathan had to say.

"You have to listen to me!" he screamed, but no one stopped to listen. "You must repent for your sins, or there will be no hope for you," he yelled as people stared at him in shock and confusion. "Sir?" Jonathan heard a voice behind him. Suddenly Jonathan turned to face an angry looking police officer. "Sir, you need to move on," he urged, but Jonathan didn't hear him.

"I'm just trying to tell these people about God. I want them to know that there is better for them if they denounce their sins!," he yelled as the Officer frowned. "If you don't move, I'm going to arrest you for trespassing," the officer responded as Jonathan shot him a confused look.

"You want to arrest me for trying to save these people?" he asked. "You're a Police Officer. You understand the law. I am trying to show these people what will happen if they don't follow God's law and you want to arrest me for that?" he asked. The Police Officer wore a look of sympathy as he shook his head at Jonathan.

"Sir, you are trespassing. The owners of this property contacted us. You're disturbing the peace right now, sir! You have to move," he said as Jonathan looked around and noticed the people walking by wearing looks of confused concern on their faces. Jonathan ignored the young police officer and raised his arms in a question to the crowd that had gathered. "Do you believe in God?" Jonathan questioned them as they shook their heads in pity at him.

No one answered him, instead they all began to talk amongst themselves. "Who among you wants to be saved?" Jonathan questioned as the faces in the crowd stared back at him in bewilderment. "Why won't they listen," Jonathan asked as he looked up to the sky, asking God for help. He saw people laughing and pointing at him like he was a joke. They treated him like he was a drunken vagrant.

Reaching down and retrieving a rock, Jonathan hurled it in their direction in frustration. "I know you hear me!" he screamed as the crowd around them began to grow. "Don't let the sun go down on your sins. God is coming to claim his faithful servants. Do you want to be lost?!" he screamed in frustration.

The Police Officer looked around nervously as he sighed in disbelief at Jonathan's behavior. "Alright, that's it," the Police Officer warned as he pulled out his handcuffs and placed them on Jonathan's wrist.

Galatians 6:1-10

"Brethren, if a man be overtaken in a fault, ye which are spiritual, restore such an one in the spirit of meekness; considering thyself, lest thou also be tempted.[2] Bear ye one another's burdens, and so fulfil the law of Christ.[3] For if a man think himself to be something, when he is nothing, he deceiveth himself.[4] But let every man prove his own work, and then shall he have rejoicing in himself alone, and not in another.

[5] For every man shall bear his own burden. [6] Let him that is taught in the word communicate unto him that teacheth in all good things."

Chapter 50

Robert glanced around the sanctuary at Living Waters Baptist Church. His heart was full of joy and peace as he sang along to hymns that he hadn't heard in over a decade. The minute he walked inside the church, a feeling of jubilation washed over him. All he could do was thank God for his life.

Although he lost his best friend and felt a miserable pang of loneliness, he was grateful for God's hand on his life. Robert knew that growing up, he had two choices. He could have chosen the other side, but he was grateful that he decided to follow God. It was his faith that kept him and his mother mentally together when his father walked out on the family.

Robert learned how to pray as a young child. Growing up with Brad was an excellent experience for a child like Robert. He and his mother attended services at the Living Waters Baptist Church once he and Brad became friends. He chose the third pew in the middle of the church.

Robert had his reasons.

He smoothed the IZOD pullover over his slacks and exhaled. Robert tried his best to calm his nerves, but it was no use. He could smell her perfume before he saw her approach, honeysuckle, and roses. She smelled like a garden of freshly cut flowers.

When he looked up, and his brown eyes met her sparkling blue eyes, he smiled instinctively. "Good morning Robert. It's great to see you again," Monica said as she sat down beside him. Monica Brogden was a gorgeous woman with long blonde curls and a laugh that bubbled like champagne. Angela introduced Robert to Monica during a Couples Ministry bowling event several months prior.

Since then, Robert and Monica had become inseparable. Robert settled into the Country Village Apartments in Redwood and Monica helped him with every step of his move. Robert smiled at Monica as they shared the hymnal, singing praises to God.

He was blessed to have Monica in his life.

A long time resident of Minnesota, Monica recently joined the Living Waters Baptist Church. Monica was a divorced mother of three. Monica's youngest son left for the military a few weeks before Robert met her.

She was happy to have Robert in her life. He was a welcome distraction from the emptiness inside her home now that her boys were gone. They both turned their attention to Pastor Luke when he approached the podium.

"God is good," Pastor Luke announced as everyone in the church applauded their agreement. "I want you to look over to your neighbor and ask if it had not been for the love of God, where would I be?" he said as a low rumble took over the congregation.

Robert looked over at Monica, and they both repeated, "If it had not been for the love of God, where would I be?" and smiled at each other. A warm feeling overtook Robert as he glanced around the congregation. Everyone inside the church looked like they had a testimony to give about God's grace. It made him feel good to know that he wasn't the only person who was in need of God's grace and mercy on a daily basis.

Pastor Luke let out a frustrated sigh. "Saints, I want you to pray for my grandson as he heads out on his mission to minister the gospel. I want you to pray that God keeps him encouraged. You know that the *effectual fervent* prayers of the righteous availeth much," he said as the congregation clapped and prayed their response.

The church quieted down as Pastor Luke led them in prayer, "Father God, we come to you today thanking you for your many blessings. We thank you for your love and understanding even when we are not understanding. I pray for healing father God. I pray for the protection of your missionaries, your saints and your servants, Father God. We need your favor to encourage and uplift them right now. Many of your servants are facing persecution and abuse. I ask that you continue to heal and encourage them as they continue to do your work," he began to pray as Robert closed his eyes.

His entire body warmed when he felt Monica grab his hand and squeeze it during the prayer.

Once the church said a collective, "Amen," the church erupted in thunderous applause and praise. The drums began to beat as the congregation began to praise God for the expected answer to their prayers.

Robert looked around the church wondering where Jonathan was. He hadn't seen Jonathan in weeks. Jonathan was always on the go, and when he returned from his trips, he preferred to rest at Angela's house. He decided to call Jonathan and check in on him.

Psalm 73:26

"My flesh and my heart faileth: but God is the strength of my heart, and my portion for ever."

Chapter 51

Anna giggled as Jonathan retold the story of how he ended up in the Roseland County Jail. "Jonathan, if I didn't pick you up from the place myself, I swear I wouldn't believe it," she said smiling. Anna was tickled by their conversation. She was also thrilled to find out that Jonathan was safe and sound. When she received the urgent collect call from the Roseland County Lockup facility, she nearly fell out of the bed.

"I just want to know what made you think a rock was going to hurt someone?" she inquired. "I wasn't trying to hurt anyone. I just wanted their attention. They called the cops on me and no one wanted to listen," Jonathan exclaimed as he tried to compose himself.

"I have never been so humiliated. I just want to spread the gospel, Anna. Is it really that hard?" he asked as she nodded. "Of course it is, Jonathan. Your walk with God is not supposed to be an easy walk. It's supposed to be riddled with deep valleys and high mountains. You're supposed to face obstacles. This is where you find God. You find God in your faith, in your trials, not in only good things," she added as he listened.

"I guess I got a little carried away." Jonathan admitted with an anxious chuckle. Anna laughed hard at Jonathan's understatement.

"Thanks for coming to get me, Anna," Jonathan said with a sad smile. "It's alright, Jonathan. We all have days where we feel misunderstood. This was all a misunderstanding. I think the Police Officer was just frustrated. He seemed to cool down after he charged you with trespassing and resisting arrest, though," she laughed.

Jonathan considered her response and couldn't help but laugh along with her. "I guess this is all pretty absurd. I got arrested for preaching the gospel. My grandfather would find humor in this...if I weren't afraid it would break his heart, I'd tell him," he said as he laughed along with Anna.

"I'm sure that Pastor Luke will understand, Jonathan," she assured. "You weren't doing anything violent. It was just a misunderstanding. You can pay the fine and push this situation right out of your mind," she offered as she drove along the highway heading towards his house.

Jonathan heard what Anna said, but he knew that if his grandfather found out about his antics, he would be disappointed. The last time Jonathan faced jail time, his grandfather was right by his side. Although Jonathan appreciated his support, he felt terrible about hurting his mentor.

He could see the look of devastation on his grandfather's face when he entered the police precinct nearly two decades prior. Jonathan never wanted to see that look on his face again. In fact, it was the imprisonment and the look on Pastor Luke's face that encouraged Jonathan to change from his rebellious ways.

At the time, Jonathan was only acting out. He missed his father, desperately and his mother was struggling through depression. He needed an outlet, which Anna offered.

Being a student from the big city, Anna was more mature than Jonathan and much more experienced. Jonathan was grateful that they both changed their ways. In the past, they found themselves in more trouble than they could handle.

"What did you tell my mother?" Jonathan questioned as the thought crossed his mind. Angela was probably beside herself at the moment. "I didn't tell your mother anything, Jonathan. After you called me, I hopped in the car and drove to bail you out of jail," she said as he laughed at the absurdity of it all.

"Man, talk about coming full circle. The last time I was in a place like the Roseland County Jail, we were locked up together for being mischievous," he chuckled as she nodded in response. "Yeah, some things never change," she said as he reached out and grabbed her hand.

"You had my back then, and you still have my back, now," Jonathan responded. "I don't know what I would do without you, Anna," he said as she smiled at him and turned her attention back to the road.

Anna didn't let on how she was feeling inside. Her heart was beating like a loud drum. Her palms were sweating. She genuinely cared for Jonathan. Anna was glad that she still holds a place in Jonathan's life. At his most desperate time, he still called on her. That made her smile broadly.

"What are you smiling about? You just bailed me out of jail?," Jonathan teased. "Don't make me take you back down there. Now you're trespassing on my nerves," Anna teased as they laughed.

"So are you going to tell me what happened to your eye and lip," she said referring to Jonathan's swollen, black eye and bruised lip. Jonathan instinctively raised a hand to his lip and winced from the pain. "Let's just say that the jail is not the best place to minister to the public," he responded as they filled the car with laughter once again.

Jonathan glanced over at his friend, watching her face brighten every time she smiled. Anna was his saving grace; his lifeline at the moment. She wasn't going to allow Jonathan to give up and that was precisely what he needed.

Jonathan was grateful for Anna. When he sat in that jail cell all he could think about were his failures and disappointments. He didn't see a way out of his situation. Jonathan's nights were tortured with visions.

Jonathan couldn't escape his purpose, even if he wanted to. He was bound to tell the world what would happen if they shunned the commandments and turned their back on God.

Jonathan made up his mind during that restless night in jail. He would do it at any cost. It didn't matter how many times he faced beatings and ridicule. He would be determined and just as steadfast as the Preachers in his visions.

His purpose was higher than his comfort.

Jonathan knew that if he didn't spread the gospel, he would suffer the consequences, but his determination to preach at any cost was actually costing him a lot. Anna sensed his inner turmoil and reached over to give Jonathan a reassuring pat on the shoulder. "It will be alright, Jonathan. It always is," she added with assurance.

She turned a devastating situation into something joyful. They were actually laughing at an event that shook Jonathan to his core.

That was Anna's power.

Romans 1:16

"For I am not ashamed of the gospel of Christ: for it is the power of God unto salvation to every one that believeth; to the Jew first, and also to the Greek."

Chapter 52

Jonathan held on tight to his two daughters as he considered the journey ahead. He was heading out to New Orleans for a few days then heading to Biloxi, Mississippi to a small church there. Although none of his church visits paid much, Jonathan was determined to go and share the gospel.

Brittany was at the age where she questioned everything. Nearly a year had passed since Kelly's death, and they were still mourning her loss. Brittany and Brianna both adjusted well. Angela made sure that they were in attendance at Sunday School and any other event the church hosted.

The girls had friends, and Jonathan was grateful to see that they were adjusting well to their new lifestyle without their mother. Every night during prayer, Brianna said a prayer for her mommy in heaven, and it crushed Jonathan inside, each time.

Brittany waited for Jonathan to respond to her question. Her bright blue eyes held a question when he hugged her. "I won't be gone long, darling," he said as he gently touched her face. "Daddy, I love you. Please be careful," she said as she gave Jonathan another hug.

Jonathan tried to assure his baby girl that he would be fine, but he understood her anxiety. The poor girl had already lost her mother, and her father was always on the move. When Jonathan returned from his trips, he was either worn out from the trip or nursing a new bruise.

Eager to spread the gospel everywhere he went, Jonathan visited the malls and crowded places often, searching for people hungry for the word. Sometimes people didn't want to hear what he had to say.

One day he stood outside the local shopping mall in Los Angeles ministering to a group of four young men when one of them spit on him. Jonathan was so taken aback he didn't know what to say. He wiped the wetness from his face with a tissue and continued to pray for the young men. Jonathan had experienced so much hatred he felt immune to it after a while.

It saddened him that no one wanted to know about Jesus. They turned their back on him and laughed at him. Jonathan was called crazy on numerous occasions, but he didn't give up. Each time he felt low and ready to give in, Anna was by his side pushing him to continue with his mission.

Pastor Luke was growing concerned about Jonathan's plight. He wanted Jonathan to stop ministering on the streets and return to the pulpit. Jonathan tried to explain to Pastor Luke that he couldn't let a day go by without spreading the word. It didn't matter where he was, he had to do so. That was when he saw the gleam of pride in his grandfather's eyes.

They prayed together. Pastor Luke continued to encourage Jonathan on his journey. He sent letters to neighboring Pastors and called on friends to see who could host his grandson. They worked together on a personal campaign to reach religious leaders around the world. Inside each personalized letter, Jonathan eloquently described what he saw in the pit.

Jonathan pleaded with the leaders to listen to him and help him spread the word about the revelations he received. While he awaited the response from leaders of the Apostolic, Baptist, and Catholic Churches, he took to the streets to share the gospel.

Jonathan received ridicule on every turn. People laughed in his face when he asked them if they believed in God. Redwood wasn't a large area, so he drove around Minnesota stopping off to pray with people and tell people about God.

The response he received was less than ideal.

Some churches agreed to let Jonathan come out to visit, but once he began speaking the truth about what was to come, they grew uncomfortable. He was asked to leave several churches. Pastor Luke was disappointed by the treatment his grandson received, but not surprised.

It had been this way since Biblical times. People would rather stick their head in the sand and forget about dangers rather than change their lifestyles. The things Jonathan preached against were enmeshed in the very souls of the world. Pastor Luke prayed that the heart's of religious leaders across the globe would soften to his grandson's message.

Jonathan sat on the Spirit Airlines flight and read the Bible. He was intrigued by Paul's struggles. Jonathan wanted to grow in his knowledge of God. Reading what Paul wrote to the church in Corinthians helped him understand that no matter what he endured it would all be for God's glory. Paul's story encouraged us that no one could move beyond God's salvation.

Jonathan gained strength and tranquility from the scriptures. "Attention Ladies and Gentlemen, we are approaching the Louis Armstrong International Airport. Flight attendants, please prepare for cross-check," the pilot announced, interrupting Jonathan's thoughts.

Jonathan was expected to preach the missionary service at Lake View Baptist Church in Harvey, Louisiana. After Jonathan located his rental car, he drove to the hotel and checked in. He was grateful that the church approved the trip as a missionary visit and paid for his travel. Jonathan hadn't returned to work since his wife's death. He couldn't bring himself to return to New York City without his wife.

Instead, Jonathan chose to work for Living Waters Baptist Church as an Administrative Assistant while he figured out his next move. Appearing at churches helped supplement his income, but not too much. He only received three invitations per month, and most churches paid him based on donations and tithes.

Even though he didn't make a great deal of money, Jonathan enjoyed what he did, and he knew that it was making a difference. Jonathan was convinced that no matter what he faced, God was right beside him, protecting him.

After he checked in to the hotel, Jonathan called Angela to check on them. "How are my favorite ladies doing?" he asked when she answered the phone. Jonathan laughed when he heard the commotion going on in the background. "We're baking cookies," Angela said as the girls cheered in the background.

"Okay, I was just checking in on you guys. I have an evening service to attend later on. I'll call you once I return to the hotel," he assured his mother. Jonathan was grateful for Angela. She stepped in the role of mother and father for Jonathan while he continued to spread the gospel. It was because of Angela that Jonathan could travel.

After he ended the call with Angela, Jonathan dialed Anna's number. "Hey, Anna," he said when she answered the phone. "Hey, Jonathan. I was just thinking about you," she said as he blushed sheepishly. "I'm glad you made it safely," she quickly added to kill the uncomfortable silence that had grown on the line.

"Yeah, I have service in an hour. I'll call you afterward," Jonathan said. "Okay, I'm leaving for Children's Choir Rehearsal," she said. "I'm sure it will run late, so how about I call you afterward," she said as he agreed to her plan. He was about to hang up the phone when he heard his name, "Jonathan?" Anna questioned. "Yes?" he asked. "I love you," she responded. "I'll see you soon," she added and ended the call as he held the phone in shock.

Galatians 6:7

"Be not deceived; God is not mocked: for whatsoever a man soweth, that shall he also reap."

Chapter 53

Dr. Lawrence Fry took a long swig out of the water jug and pushed the lush green palm out of his way. Sounds of crickets, creatures, and leaves rustling under the gentle breeze provided the perfect soundtrack to the trek.

He continued walking behind the guide, trying to keep up with the long legs of the man he grew to know as Hindolo. Burning desperation propelled his journey. He wasn't worried about the supremely scenic views that he rushed beyond. Like always, Dr. Fry was in search of a treasure.

Although he was a very wealthy man, Dr. Fry's greed pushed him to places that had no bounds. He knew that what he did teeter on the line of criminal but Dr. Fry convinced himself that he was committing charitable acts.

In his mind, he was helping to enrich local tribes and communities with knowledge and spoils from the Western world. Dr. Fry was exposing these savages to civilized life. He reasoned that the locals should have felt grateful to work with him. He provided many people with their first glimpse of a cell phone or a tablet. Dr. Fry took pictures with Kings who he gifted iPads and headphones too for access to their ancient sites. Many people were easily persuadable, his only concern was the few who didn't care about money or materials. They were the toughest to get around.

Luckily, he brought back up. Dr. Fry touched his right pant leg to ensure that his gun was still securely in place. Sometimes the toughest shells required a weapon to crack.

Dr. Fry wasn't afraid to use force on anyone to get what he needed. He stopped short of killing someone on several occasions, but luckily he was able to intimidate tribal members into letting him have his way.

Nearly twenty years later, Lawrence Fry still felt the constant aching of guilt. He couldn't get Brad out of his mind. Lawrence couldn't see Pastor Luke Flannigan on television or streamed without weeping in sadness for what he'd done.

Lawrence tried to pretend like the only thing that mattered to him was money, but even he had a heart. Raised in a Southern Baptist household, Lawrence knew all too well about sin, repentance, and redemption. He knew that God was forgiving, but he wasn't sure if forgiveness was something he actually deserved.

Brad haunted Lawrence's dreams.

He was awakened every night with horrible visions. The day he killed Brad played in his dreams every time he closed his eyes. Lawrence sought therapy for his night frights but how could he tell someone what he did? He would be locked away forever if he confessed about Brad's murder.

In one of his weaker moments, Lawrence wrote a letter to Pastor Luke Flannigan detailing what he did and why. Lawrence rationalized that if he wrote down his thoughts, his pain it would somehow disappear from his mind.

Lawrence found himself writing every night. Over the 19 years since Brad's death, he had amassed quite a stock of writings. He wrote letters to Angela, Jonathan and Pastor Flannigan apologizing for what he'd done to destroy their family. Lawrence cried and prayed for forgiveness every night, but he knew in his heart that he had to make things right.

He just didn't know how. Lawrence tried to clear his mind by keeping in close pace behind Hindolo.

His guide, Hindolo was being compensated triple his asking price, just to lead him to a treasured find. Dr. fry sought out a valuable jewel. One of the largest pieces of topaz ever located. The treasure was held, securely, in a mine 50 miles east of Sierra Leone. Dr. Fry had already bribed the security guard on duty for the shift. He would just walk in and walk out with his treasure.

Dr. Fry paid a hefty price for his current mission. The mine he planned to visit was protected by a fiercely defensive local tribe. The warnings didn't deter him, however. Dr. Fry was used to intimidating locals and savages. He knew how to deal with them. Money was a beautiful thing.

He reasoned that most people didn't realize how easy it was to win over someone by merely offering them a gift. Dr. Fry used this knowledge as his key into many protected areas. He was required to pay fines and fees to merely enter the area where he could locate his guide.

"For as much money as I've shelled out to make it here...one would expect not to forget to purchase their mosquito spray," he said swatting at the mosquitoes as his guide continued to walk without a response. Hindolo didn't mind the bugs. He too was on a mission. The hefty salary that he was paid would help secure the needs of his family for years to come.

His wife was pregnant with their third child. He couldn't wait to move his family out of his childhood home. They had been living there for nearly six years. Hindolo prayed every night for a miracle. Then, several weeks ago he received a message from Dr. Fry.

He couldn't believe it. His prayers had been answered. Hindolo didn't tell his wife about his journey. Instead, he wanted to surprise her with their new home once the baby was born. He figured one trek out to the jungle with Dr. Fry, and he would earn enough to not only purchase and decorate his home, but he could also save for a rainy day. Hindolo was beside himself.

All he had to do was lead Dr. Fry through the jungle to the mine. Dr. Fry would take it from there. Lawrence Fry instructed Hindolo that once he secured the location, he would be free to leave. Hindolo sensed no danger in his journey but brought along his knife and pistol just in case.

As they reached the mine, Dr. Fry let out a yelp. He was thrilled to have the help of Hindolo. The tunnel was difficult to locate. Dr. Fry illegally obtained the map, and Hindolo interpreted it. Together the men followed the instructions from the ancient map Dr. Fry clutched tightly.

Dr. Fry was so engulfed in his map he didn't see the two native warriors approach until they were too close. One of the decorated warriors pulled out a knife and slit Dr. Fry's throat from behind. In the middle of the minefield, surrounded by lush jungle, Dr. Fry paid the ultimate price for his greed.

Hindolo began to walk towards the jungle, unharmed, having completed his mission.

Ecclesiastes 4:8-9

"There is one alone, and there is not a second; yea, he hath neither child nor brother: yet is there no end of all his labour; neither is his eye satisfied with riches; neither saith he, For whom do I labour, and bereave my soul of good? This is also vanity, yea, it is a sore travail. [9] Two are better than one; because they have a good reward for their labour."

Chapter 54

Anna and Jonathan stood nervously while Pastor Luke Flannigan read a beautiful poem written by Monica Brogden. Monica was a lovely poet who the church had grown to love. She wrote poems to accompany the Sunday church bulletin for every service. As a school librarian, Monica spent a great deal of time between the pages of a great book. Her poems were striking and profound.

Robert knew about her love for poetry and literature. That's the chief reason why he proposed to his beloved at the Hennepin County Library. The most extensive library in Minnesota. To Monica's delight and surprise, Robert managed to have a pianist play her favorite song, "Beethoven's Symphony No 5" as he dropped down to one knee. Jonathan, Anna, and Angela were in attendance, as well.

Throughout several months, Robert began to find his comfort zone in Minnesota. He owed it all to Jonathan and the rest of the Flannigan family. They welcomed him into their lives with open arms. Robert finally had the family that he prayed to God for. Even when Robert was a young child, he felt lonely.

Although he didn't talk about his private life often, Robert was plagued by the troubles of his youth. In fact, his youth prevented him from establishing many sustainable relationships. His father didn't have much time for him, and his mother battled with a crippling depression. This left Robert alone, often.

He was happy to finally have a family.

Jonathan was equally as gratified for Robert's presence in his life. Robert became Jonathan's mentor and wise counsel. While he still went to his grandfather for Biblical wisdom, it was nice to talk to someone closer to his age about certain things. Pastor Luke was an awesome grandfather, but some things Jonathan struggled to help him understand. There was a slight age barrier that neither men recognized.

Robert helped to round out their group. The three men became the three musketeers. Jonathan, Robert and Pastor Luke spent their lazy Saturday afternoons fishing together. Sometimes they swapped stories about Brad, taking turns sharing his jokes.

Jonathan glanced at his grandfather. He looked like a slightly older version of Brad Flannigan. The man that he teased as an "Old Man" could still outrun him in a race. Jonathan even depended on his grandfather for his wisdom and to help when his faith was low.

It pained him to see his grandfather without a wife. As long as Jonathan could remember his grandfather was fully immersed in the church. He tried to talk him into dating, but Pastor Luke was more focused on gaining more souls for the Kingdom.

The church gave him peace and comfort. Pastor Luke said that he couldn't imagine remarrying after his wife died. Jonathan thought about his conversation with Pastor Luke about remarrying after the death of a spouse. It was an awkward conversation. Pastor Luke encouraged Jonathan to head out into the dating world as soon as he felt ready. He wanted Jonathan to find love again. Jonathan just didn't understand why his grandfather didn't take his own advice.

Pastor Luke was a healthy, fit man who didn't look a year over 40. His face was smooth, and if it weren't for the full head of white hair covering his head, many would have mistaken him for Brad. Jonathan had to admit that Pastor Luke looked dapper in a black tuxedo at the request of the lovely bride, Monica.

"Ladies and Gentlemen, I present to you Mr. and Mrs. Robert Christian Wellington III," Pastor Luke said as the entire congregation cheered and clapped for the newlywed couple.

Monica's face beamed with joy and Robert looked as proud as a peacock. Jonathan wished that his father was there to witness the moment that he and Robert had fussed over for weeks.

"Congratulations, Bro," Jonathan said as he gave Robert a firm pat on the back. Robert looked like he was going to faint under the hot lights of the center stage. It was all too comical for Jonathan. He remembered how he felt on his wedding day. He couldn't wait to marry Kelly, they were engaged for over a year. Jonathan recalled that once he entered the church, a desperate urge to bolt hit him.

He looked around the immaculately decorated sanctuary. Everything was covered in white. The mahogany brown church pews were draped with white fabric. Hanging high above the happy couple was a sparkly crystal chandelier. White roses and crystal adorned every square inch of the building. It was all a lovely scene.

Jonathan laughed as Robert shot him a wink and a mischievous smile. His eyes met Anna's as they both blushed and looked away.

2 Timothy 3:12-17

"Yea, and all that will live godly in Christ Jesus shall suffer persecution.[13] But evil men and seducers shall wax worse and worse, deceiving, and being deceived.[14] But continue thou in the things which thou hast learned and hast been assured of, knowing of whom thou hast learned them; [15] And that from a child thou hast known the holy scriptures, which are able to make thee wise unto salvation through faith which is in Christ Jesus. [16] All scripture is given by inspiration of God, and is profitable for doctrine, for reproof, for correction, for instruction in righteousness: [17] That the man of God may be perfect, thoroughly furnished unto all good works."

Epilogue

Jonathan drove to the hotel trying his best to conceal his frustration. The congregants at the church laughed at him and called him a liar when he told them what was revealed to him. Jonathan was so sick and tired of being considered crazy for warning everyone.

He was encouraged to see that a few of the congregants tried to hear him out. Out of the 200 in attendance at the large auditorium sized building in Harvey, Louisiana only thirty remained after Jonathan spoke. Although it was unnerving to witness people stand up and walk away in the middle of his sermon, Jonathan didn't mind.

It was the ridicule and the accusations that he minded.

Jonathan stood in shock as a male congregant reared back in his seat and yelled at him. Jonathan was speaking on the sins of fornication. The young member accused Jonathan of being a hypocrite when he encouraged the younger members to abstain from sexual encounters until marriage.

Jonathan simply told the person that he would pray for them. He admitted that his life was not perfect. He confessed of his sins in the church just so no one would be confused about his plight.

"I'm not here to show you how righteous I am," he said as several members pursed their lips and rolled their eyes at him. "I just want to save you all from eternal damnation. The days of revelation are at hand. We are living it right now. I want to warn you and help you get the word out to warn others," he pleaded, but no one wanted to hear him.

As the members began to funnel out of the church, he caught a glimpse of the Pastor standing in the back of the church. The older gentleman looked like he would have rather been anywhere else besides there at that moment.

Jonathan felt so discouraged. He couldn't wait to get out of the church. As he drove down I10 in Louisiana, he began to pray to God for direction. Jonathan was in search of guidance or meaning behind the pain and heartache he'd experienced.

Since he made the decision to minister the gospel, Jonathan had lost his wife, his career, his home, his independence, countless friends, and he was slowly losing his faith.

He and Anna decided to keep their relationship strictly platonic. Anna felt uncomfortable starting a romantic relationship with him after knowing and loving Kelly. While she loved Jonathan, it didn't feel right to her. It was too complicated for Anna. Although, they said that their relationship wouldn't change, Jonathan felt the tension whenever they were close.

Life just didn't seem the same to Jonathan anymore. His daughters, his mother, and his grandfather were the only reason why he arose every morning to continue on with his mission.

It was starting to become too much for the young man.

There were many times when Jonathan considered packing up his belongings and returning to the city and his old life. Jonathan knew that he could regain his law career and open his practice. It wouldn't have been too farfetched from his life's goals, anyway. He was ready now to return to his old life.

The life of a missionary was wearing on his spirit. He wasn't received well. Most people treated him like a vagrant, begging for money. They treated him like he wanted something from them. All he wanted was their salvation!

It frustrated Jonathan because all he wanted was to save them all. None of them tried to save themselves. "Lord what else must I endure before I can be made whole, again," he pleaded.

Jonathan was tired and weary.

He missed his daughters. Angela had taken over most of the responsibilities of caring for his daughters, mainly since he chose the route of a missionary. Jonathan was on the road more than he had ever been and he was losing steam.

Jonathan absently made a left turn on Slidell Avenue and pulled into the local 7-eleven for a soda to boost his spirits. Once he entered the store, he noticed a disheveled teenager standing in front of the store, gazing at the magazines absentmindedly. The boy looked just about as tired as Jonathan felt. Judging by his appearance, he looked like he was a person who lived on the streets. Jonathan paid for his soda and then made his way over to the teen.

"God bless you, young man. Can I buy you something to eat?" he asked the young man who eagerly nodded as Jonathan went to retrieve a hot dog and chips from the counter clerk. He paid for the meal and took it to the teenager who eagerly accepted it. "God bless you," the teen said to Jonathan, which instantly warmed his heart. Jonathan left the store and headed to his car. Once he reached the door, he felt someone approach him from behind.

"Give me your wallet" the gruff voice grumbled as Jonathan fumbled with his keys to hand it to the tall man standing too close to him. "I said give it to me. What are you looking at me for?" the man demanded as Jonathan responded. "I'm sorry. Here" Jonathan said reaching for his wallet.

"Hey get out of here!" a voice called out in the distance. Suddenly, Jonathan heard a loud gunshot and then his assailant bolted down the street. Instinctively, Jonathan turned away from his car and started running. He chased the assailant for a few yards before his legs grew heavy. Jonathan collapsed to the ground as everything around him began to spin, rapidly.

"What is going on?" he asked as he suddenly felt a burning pain in his chest. He reached down and placed his hand directly under his left breast bone. When he brought his hands to his face, Jonathan smelled the familiar scent of blood.

"Hold on, sir. I'm calling for help now!" he heard someone call out from the distance as he tried to stand and face the voice. "No, sir don't move. You've been shot! We have to get help for you!" Jonathan heard someone say.

"Oh God! There's so much blood" he heard as his eyes grew heavy. "Sir, don't close your eyes!" a loud voice cried. "Sir, do you hear me?" someone asked.

Jonathan didn't respond.

He couldn't.

Everything went black.

When Jonathan opened his eyes again the entire room was white and covered in bright light. He had to shield his eyes from the brightness. He struggled for a moment to stand to his feet, but when he finally stood, he gasped in surprise. He was no longer in New Orleans, it felt like he was no longer on Earth. "Where am I?" he asked as he looked around the soft white room.

Jonathan walked until he reached a large golden throne. He stood back and stared at it in wonder. He knew exactly where he was, and suddenly he felt like he was back at home. "Well done thy good and faithful servant," the booming yet comforting voice said as the gates of heaven opened wide for Jonathan.

He smiled with amazement. "It's over?" he asked. "But God, I didn't get to warn enough people," he said. "I don't feel like my job is done," he said as a feeling of unworthiness washed over him. "Nonsense," the booming voice responded as visions began to appear in front of Jonathan.

Jonathan wiped away tears of sadness as he witnessed visions of the Earth under extreme war and famine. He saw millions of people dying. He watched as the seals were broken and he knew that the book of Revelations was in full effect.

Jonathan wept at the death and destruction of the Earth and its inhabitants. He felt a sinking in his stomach. He wished that he could have warned more people. Jonathan's eyes moist with tears he asked God, "is this the beginning of the end of the earth?"

We invite you to continue your journey with the

"Behind the Door Trilogy," during my weekly Podcast.

Visit www.drhlbarner.com

- Receive an update on the Behind the Door Trilogy adventure to reach the New York Times Best seller and movie offers. Register your email address with us today.

- Purchases additional copies of Behind the Door and share with your family and friends. Please your thoughts about "What if there is No God and What if there is a God? Help me expand this global conversation. Share with Churches, Book Clubs, Homes, Families, Universities, Seminaries, and other organizations.

- Tune in to Dr. Honney Lavern Barner's Hour of Power (HoP) weekly Podcast. Discussions about Behind the Door Trilogy – What if there was no God and What if there is a God?

- Visit our Facebook page, Twitter, Instagram, and LinkedIn.

- Visit drhlbarner.com to read my recent blog, My Faith, Radio Show, Books, Author Information and much more. Don't forget to leave your email address

- Sign up for my monthly newsletter.

- Message the Author and get updates on Behind the Door Trilogy

- Post your thoughts, insights, and testimonies about Behind the Door Trilogy on all your Social Media resources.

- Read what others around the world are saying about the Behind the Door Trilogy.

- All the profits from the sale of my novels will be used to fund the movie "Behind the Door". Please order the entire Behind the Door Trilogy. Help me raise funds to produce a movie by hosting fundraising events anywhere and everywhere.

Word of mouth - Matters

Our goal for Behind the Door Trilogy is to become #1 on the New York Times Bestseller's list simply by inspired, passionate, and motivated readers and supporters spreading the word about this life changing novel.

We need your help in spreading the word to everyone you know and everyone you don't know. Here are some ideas on how you can help get the word out to your circle of friends.

Talk about "Behind the Door" on **Email, Twitter, Instagram, Facebook, You Tube, Messenger,** and blogs. Host discussion forums you visit, and other places you engage other people on the Internet. I am not asking you to post advertisements, simply share your thoughts on how after reading it, made you feel and share the link to" Behind the Door" website.

Purchase a few books as gifts and donate them to churches, shelters, prisons, rehabilitation homes, and other places where people may need to be encouraged about their faith.

If you own a small business please consider putting a display of this novel on your counter to resell to customers. We offer discounts for resale for orders of 10 or more novels.

If you have a **Website, Blog, You Tube Channel**, etc. please consider sharing "Behind the Door" and tell them how it impacted you and your faith. Don't tell them how the story ends but do give them the link to the website - **www.drhlbarner.com.**

Write a **book review and publish it in your local newspaper, magazine, or website**. Contact your local radio, podcast or TV station to have the author on their show.

Give "Behind the Door" as a gift for **Birthdays, Christmas, Anniversaries, Fundraisers, Give-a-ways** and other events where gifts and prizes are expected.

Make recommendations to community groups, church groups, book clubs, and others to have the author as their guest speaker at your conventions, seminars, Expos, festivals, and other gatherings.

Use "Behind the Door" for **Small groups discussions at your local Church and Book clubs.** The author would be honored to make a surprise appearance.

Insights to Upcoming

Behind the Door III: "Revelation Unleashed"

Release in 2020

The third installation in the *Behind the Door* series begins with God telling Jonathan that it is time that his Son, Jesus, return to Earth to gather the Church and prepare the Earth for His eternal dwelling place.

At this point, *Behind the Door III – Revelation Unleashed* will follow the actual book of Revelation through the eyes of "John" as written.

Will Jonathan be the replacement for "John" from the book of Revelation?

What will God allow Jonathan to see? Is this the actual end of the Earth as we know it? What will be unleashed upon the Earth? What is happening upon the Earth that has angered God to this end?

DR. BARNER'S HOUR OF POWER

$A+C=x^2$ $E=mc^2$

E Plubirus Unum

$|x-a|=a^2-x^2$